Wendy Dunham

HARVEST HOUSE PUBLISHERS
EUGENE, OREGON

Scripture verses are taken from

The New King James Version®. Copyright © 1982 by Thomas Nelson, Inc. Used by permission. All rights reserved.

The *Holy Bible*, New Living Translation, copyright ©1996, 2004, 2007, 2013 by Tyndale House Foundation. Used by permission of Tyndale House Publishers, Inc., Carol Stream, Illinois 60188. All rights reserved.

The ESV® Bible (The Holy Bible, English Standard Version®), copyright © 2001 by Crossway, a publishing ministry of Good News Publishers. Used by permission. All rights reserved.

Cover by Writely Designed, Buckley, Washington

Cover photo © altanaka / Fotolia

Published in association with William K. Jensen Literary Agency, 119 Bampton Court, Eugene, Oregon 97404.

MY NAME IS RIVER

Copyright © 2015 Wendy Dunham
Published by Harvest House Publishers
Eugene, Oregon 97402
www.harvesthousepublishers.com

Library of Congress Cataloging-in-Publication Data
    Dunham, Wendy.
    My name is River / Wendy Dunham.
        pages cm
    Summary: River Starling, adopted under mysterious circumstances, has lived most of her eleven years on her grandparents' Pennsylvania farm but after Gram suddenly decides they must move to Birdsong, West Virginia, River finds an unlikely new friend, learns about God's love, and begins to feel at home.
    ISBN 978-0-7369-6461-6 (pbk.)
    ISBN 978-0-7369-6462-3 (eBook)
    [1. Moving, Household—Fiction. 2. Grandmothers—Fiction. 3. Friendship—Fiction. 4. Christian life—Fiction. 5. Adoption—Fiction. 6. Missing persons—Fiction. 7. West Virginia—History—20th century—Fiction.] I. Title.
    PZ7.1.D86My 2015
    [Fic]—dc23

                                                                         2014040664

Printed in the United States of America

            18 19 20 21 22 23 / BP-JH / 10 9 8 7 6 5 4 3 2

For Erin and Evan,
who are the most loved, adored,
and amazing children I could have ever hoped for.
I am so very grateful for you.

✳ ✳ ✳

Acknowledgments

Heartfelt thanks to Ruth Samsel, my delightful agent, who believed in River right from the start.

And to Barb Sherrill, Peggy Wright, and everyone else at Harvest House who wrapped their arms around River and me and made us feel like family.

Before Ruth, Barb, and Peggy, there were others who provided inspiration—various writing friends, members of Rochester Area Children's Writers & Illustrators (RACWI) and WNY Word Weavers, and most notably my friend Wendy Dunn of Paper Dance Editing.

A big shout-out to Sam Files, a preteen and lover of books who, after reading an early draft, said, "This is the best story ever. I read it three times!" That was the fuel I needed. Thank you, Sam.

And to my parents, family, and friends I've known over the years, I thank you. For without you, I'd be empty and have no stories to share.

* ✶ * ✶ * ✶ . * ✶ * ✶ . * ✶ * ✶ * ✶ . * ✶ * ✶ . * ✶

1

Moving Day

on't you worry now, Sugar Pie. Everything's gonna be all right." Gram must've said that a million times over the last few days, and that's a pretty big promise to make to a grandkid.

But, truthfully, I don't think I've ever doubted her because Gram doesn't lie. She says, "Life ain't worth a hill of beans if you don't speak the truth." And in Gram's book, even a half-truth measures up to a whole lie. But today, the day we're moving, I'm working hard at believing her.

Gram's in the kitchen double-checking our cupboards. She said the only thing she's leaving behind is mouse poop (not that I'd ever seen any). The cupboard doors bang as she yells up the stairs. "Label them boxes, Sugar Pie, with your name and what you got in 'em."

Packing's a lot harder than I thought. Not the actual packing, that's easy, but the part about leaving everything behind. This old brick farmhouse is all I've ever known or at least all I can remember.

I push the last box to the middle of my room and write big black letters on the side:

River's Box
pillow
red flannel blanket

hockey pucks
baseball glove
ballerina jewelry box

I think about leaving the jewelry box behind but don't because it's from Gram. Plus that's where I keep my heart necklace.

My real name is River, but Gram calls me "Sugar Pie." I've been alive for four thousand six hundred and twenty days, which means I'll be thirteen on my next birthday, and in all that time, I still haven't figured out why anyone would name their kid River. But that's the name I came with—to my adoptive parents, anyways. I thought babies were supposed to come into the world free of names and everything, but I came fully clothed, wearing a white and yellow checkered dress just the right size for an eighteen-month-old. And I only know that because Gram told me.

Gram said she was blown clear out of the water on the day my parents brought me home. She had no idea they were going to adopt. It was like I'd fallen straight from the sky, and when I asked why I was such a secret, she shook her head and said, "Sugar Pie, I haven't a clue. Your mother never did have the sense God gave a goose."

Gram keeps a special picture of me on her nightstand. It's the picture she took that day. My mom (who is Gram's daughter) is holding me on her hip, and my dad (Gram's son-in-law) is standing behind with his arms wrapped around the both of us. I was actually cute—real chubby with a crooked little smile. Even then I had a ton of hair. It was curly all over the place and shiny brown like a chestnut. Hanging around my neck was a silver necklace with a dangling heart charm. On the front "River" was engraved, and on the back was 9-23-1970. I didn't come with a birth certificate, which Gram said was the most ridiculous thing she'd ever heard. A lot has changed since then. First of all, I'm not chubby anymore. And second of all, my mom and dad are gone.

As far as my real parents go, I can pretty much guess I came to them the way most any kid does—plopped into the hands of a doctor, screaming at the top of my lungs, and completely naked. And since they gave me away when I was only one and a half, I can only guess I was unlovable too.

After I was adopted, Gram said my parents loved me more than all the frogs in the pond. But after six months, when I was two, they decided I was too much trouble. That's when they packed everything important into the trunk of their Mustang and drove away.

They didn't pack me.

But Gram said I wasn't any more trouble than Mud Pie, the three-legged pig she had at the time. She said I was just like any other two-year-old who liked getting into things and had to throw a hissy fit every now and then. Gram said my parents never could figure out what they wanted. She spent years trying to find them but then decided it was time to give up.

I have no idea how one kid could have two sets of parents, and in two short years, have them both decide they don't want you anymore. Maybe I really was too much trouble, but I've never heard Gram tell a lie or anything even close.

It's been ten years, and they haven't come back.

Sometimes I imagine my parents on the day they left. They're cruising along in their Mustang, singing along with The Beach Boys without a care in the world. My mom leans her head against my dad's shoulder (the one tattooed with a heart and her name inside), and she's dangling her feet out the window, letting the wind tickle her toes. She smiles and turns to check on me. That's when she realizes I'm not there. She screams, and when my dad realizes what's going on, he does a crazy U-turn and races back home at one hundred and ten miles per hour. They run into the house all frantic, and Mom's crying uncontrollably. She picks me up, holds me tight, and says, "River, thank God you're all right! I thought Daddy put you in the backseat. You're such a good little girl and never make a peep. I thought you were just sleeping, but when I turned to check on you, I realized you weren't."

Then I realize I'm daydreaming again.

* * *

I tuck my diary deep inside the box, right between my pillow and red flannel blanket. Even though I never write in it, I think it's a good idea to save just in case. Plus, that's where I keep one of Paddles's white feathers (Paddles was the best pet duck anyone could've had).

Gram yells up the stairs again. "Hurry yourself along, Sugar Pie. You gotta be a little quicker than a herd of turtles! The movers are here."

I tape the box shut and look out my window. I say goodbye to our backyard, to the pond where I play hockey in the winter, to the creek where I caught pollywogs, and to the path leading to our woods, right where I buried Paddles. I touch the window, taking one last look at my tire swing. I remember the day Gramp hung it. He let me pick the tree. I chose the biggest oak tree right in the middle of our yard. Gramp even let me help tie the knots.

I have no idea what I'll see from my new window, but I know it won't be as beautiful as this.

2

It's Gonna Be All Right

I sit on the front steps, waiting for the movers to finish their job, and whisper goodbye to the eighteen maple trees standing tall and proud along our driveway. Gramp planted them way before I was born. They got to live longer than he did (which I hardly think is fair). But at least I've climbed to the top of every one of them—even with my eyes closed. The people who bought our house have a boy my age, but I can promise he won't climb as high as me.

When the movers are done loading Tilly, Gram's '62 Chevy pickup, Gram and I hop in and head down our driveway for the last time. Gram loves her Chevy so much she named it. She says anything so shiny and turquoise that shimmers in the sun like it does is truly alive. Gram decided on the name Tilly. And even though Tilly's been around for more than twenty years, you'd be hard up to find a speck of rust on her. And according to Gram, "Everybody ought to have a pickup cuz you never know what you'll have to haul."

We reach the end of our road when I see a beautiful lady out walking her dog. She's tall, skinny, and has a ton of curly brown hair, just like me. Maybe she's my real mom. She could've gotten pregnant when she was a teenager and then left me on the front steps of an orphanage. Maybe she never told anyone about me, which would explain why I don't have a birth certificate. Things like that can happen.

"Gram," I say, "are you sure we have to move?"

She gives me a look that says I've asked that question one too many times. "Sugar Pie, that farmhouse is too big for the two of us. It's time for moving on. Doesn't mean it's gonna be better or worse—just different." Gram takes a deep breath and lets it out real slow. "Everything's gotta change sometime, and there's not a soul on this earth that can do a thing about it."

"But what about Gramp? What do you think he'd say? And," I say as a reminder (just in case she forgot), "we won't be able to have picnics with him in the cemetery anymore."

"Don't you worry about that, Sugar Pie. All that's left of Gramp in that cemetery is a box of dry, dusty bones. The living part of him, all them memories we've got in our hearts, they're gonna travel with us anywhere we go."

We reach the freeway, head south, and pass that familiar big, green sign:

Thanks for visiting Punxsutawney, Pennsylvania,

home of Punxsutawney Phil.

Come back soon!

I stare out Tilly's window and can't look at Gram, or she'll see my eyes all watery. "But when Mom and Dad come back, they're not going to know where I am." I try to swallow the lump in my throat. "Did you even think about that?"

Gram doesn't answer right away. Maybe she doesn't know what to say. Maybe she doesn't believe they're coming back.

"Sugar Pie, I know you're worried. But you gotta remember that we haven't seen hide nor hair of your folks in over ten years. That's a mighty long time. Now, if something changes and they do come back, they'll check in with the postmaster. He'll have our new address." Gram stops talking for a minute, like she's thinking about what to say. "And when you think about how big the world is, Birdsong, West Virginia's just a hop-skip-and-a-toad's-jump away from Punxsutawney." She turns to look at me (I can tell because I see her reflection in Tilly's window). Then she pats my leg and says, "Don't you worry now, Sugar Pie. Everything's gonna be all right."

"But, Gram, couldn't we have at least waited 'til school's out? There's only a few weeks left."

Gram looks at me like she wants to say she understands or maybe that she's sorry. But she doesn't. "I know, Sugar Pie, but we've got to move now cuz I've heard the wind. And there ain't nobody who can fight the wind."

It wasn't long after Gramp died when Gram started up with the whole wind idea. One day she walked to the end of the driveway to get our mail and heard a kitten meowing. Hiding by the side of the road was a small gray kitten. Gram said it was no bigger than a ball of yarn and cuter than a bug's ear. Then Gram told me she got this funny feeling inside, like she was hearing a tender voice telling her to pick the kitten up and bring it home. Gram told herself it was hogwash and that the kitten surely belonged to someone. She told herself it would find its way home, so she left it there. But when Gram was halfway back to our house, she heard the sound of brakes screeching and a thud that nearly tore her heart in two. That night she didn't sleep a wink.

Gram had the same thing happen another time when we were heading out to buy groceries. She was backing Tilly down our driveway when she heard that tender voice again (that's when she decided to call it "the wind"). It told her to go back and lock the house. But Gram hadn't locked the house since the day she and Gramp bought it nearly fifty years before. She said there was no use wasting time doing something senseless and never went back to lock up. When we got home, our door was wide open, and anything worth a penny was gone. Gram said she learned an important lesson that day, and I knew it had nothing to do with locking a door.

I suppose since Gram heard the wind telling us to move, we're better off moving a few weeks before school's over than to stay and find out what would happen if we didn't.

Gram cracks her window, and part of her hair falls loose from her bun. As the wind pulls it out the window, it looks like a long, silver streamer waving goodbye to Punxsutawney.

Next thing I know, Gram reaches in her purse and takes out her pack of Camels. I can't stand breathing in all that smoke. It makes me feel like someone's stuffed fifty-seven cotton balls down my throat. I turn and look at Gram. "You need a smoke already?"

She keeps her eyes on the road and doesn't blink. A minute later she says, "Humph. You're right, Sugar Pie." Then without looking, she hands me her cigarettes. "Toss 'em out the window. I'm going cold turkey. It's high time for change."

"Are you serious, Gram?"

"Never been more serious in my life. Besides, they're just a pack of skinny, white rodents. You light 'em up, and their eyes glow red. You suck 'em in, and they head straight for your lungs. Then they gnaw away on them like they was hunks of provolone cheese." She grabs Tilly's steering wheel even tighter and keeps right on driving. "I'm plum done."

I open my window and toss them out, one by one, real slow—not in case she changes her mind, but in case I need to get back home. I'll follow our trail.

We drive a while longer when I decide I really ought to know something about where we're moving (and this time I'll listen). "So why'd you pick Birdsong, anyways? Didn't you say it was a small town?"

"Sure did. That's one of the things I like about it. Everyone knows everyone in a small town. Plus, the name Birdsong is so full of life it could make a dead man dance. Soon as I saw it on the map, I knew that's where we were going." Gram tucks the gray streamer back in her bun. "And," she says, "the wind told me."

Gram keeps talking, giving me all kinds of information about Birdsong. Some of it I'm sure I could do without. "And it's smack-dab in the middle of all kinds of mountains, roaring rivers, and nature parks, and it's high time we had ourselves some adventure. White-water rafting, hiking, and fishing in those ice-cold mountain streams, we're gonna do it all."

I'm beginning to think Gram might have been sucked up by aliens and returned with someone else's innards. "Gram," I say, "did you forget about your leg?"

"No siree, Sugar Pie! I didn't. There's ways around nearly everything if you put your mind to it. I'm gonna get me some physical therapy soon as we settle in. I've walked with this old Louisiana limp long enough, and it's time for change." Gram smiles bigger than I've ever seen. "And I might start plucking me a few strings on a banjo. Bluegrass music is big around those parts." Gram gives me a wink with her right eye. "I've got a feeling bigger than any twenty-pound rump roast that we were meant for this journey."

3

* *

New Kid

It's pitch black and way past ten o'clock by the time we reach our new house. We open Tilly's doors and climb out onto the gravel driveway.

"Well, Sugar Pie," Gram says, "what do you think?"

The quarter moon lets me see as much as I want. "It looks like a box with a roof...nothing like our farmhouse."

Gram comes over and pulls me close. "Like I said, Sugar Pie, it's not gonna be better or worse, just different. Besides, it's a roof over the head. What more does a sugar pie need?"

I think about saying, "Just my parents," but I don't.

Gram leans back and tilts her head to the sky. "Look at all those stars a twinkling, Sugar Pie. There won't be precipitation tonight, and good old Tilly will guard our belongings, so let's find our pillows and catch a wink on the living room floor."

"So we'll unload in the morning?"

"Not you, Sugar Pie. You'll be in school. Me and Tilly will drive around town looking to hire an extra hand."

"I can help. It won't hurt if I miss one day."

"There's nothing so important as a good education, and I'm not letting my Sugar Pie miss out."

* * *

The next morning Gram drops me off in front of Birdsong Middle School, an old two-story, brick building covered with vines. The sign out front reads "Home of the Falcons." And on account of our oversleeping (and my missing the bus), I'm late. But it doesn't bother me any. I was never in a hurry to get here in the first place. But then I remind myself that this is only for three weeks. And three weeks is doable.

Gram leans over and gives me a smooch on my cheek. "Don't you worry now, Sugar Pie," she says. "Everything's gonna be all right. Now you go on and have a good day of learning." Then she and Tilly drive away.

Two huge white pillars on each side of the front steps do their best to welcome me. But any ounce of welcomeness I might have felt disappears the second I step inside. Hanging from the ceiling directly over me is a huge falcon with its wings spread wide and its talons ready to snare me. Of course it's dead and stuffed, but, really, this is no way to welcome a new kid.

I follow the sign to the office where I'm greeted by Mr. Augur. I know that's his name because of his name tag. He seems pretty old (and short) to be a principal, and for some reason, he seems extremely eager to meet me. Then I realize it's just because his head is positioned way out in front of his body (I'm sure he doesn't hold it out there on purpose. It's just because he's old). His back is scrunched up too, which makes him look even shorter than he really is. Now I know full well it's not right to criticize his body because he obviously can't help it, but I can't help thinking that he has a very strong resemblance to a vulture.

Mr. Augur stretches his hand toward me, and since I don't want to be considered rude—in addition to being late—on my first day, I reach forward to shake it. I tell myself to be careful when I shake his hand because old people have brittle bones and they break easy. And Mr. Augur looks brittle.

He grabs my hand harder than I expected. "Welcome to Bird-song Middle School, River." Then he covers his mouth and tries clearing a frog from his throat. "I'm sure you'll like it here," he garbles.

Now, right away I'm not sure I can trust him. How does he know I'll like it? He doesn't even know me. He should've said, "I bet you're going to like it," or "I hope you'll like it." Then maybe I'd trust him.

He presses a peel-and-stick name tag on my shirt and gets so close I smell mothballs (which is probably coming from his wool coat because old people like putting mothballs in their closet).

On my name tag, RIVER STARLING is spelled out all in capital letters. Gram's last name is Nuthatch, just like Gramp's was. So that was my mom's last name too. But when she married my dad, she got his name and became a Starling. Even though Gram took me over, she decided I ought to keep Starling as my last name. I'm glad about that for two reasons. First, because everyone needs something from their past to hold onto, and second, because I don't think I could've handled a name like River Nuthatch.

I really don't want to wear this name tag. It just makes me stand out even more. It's hard enough being new. I might as well carry a neon sign that says, "Hey, look at me! I'm the new kid."

Mr. Augur guides me out of the office. "First I'll give you a tour of our school, and then I'll show you your locker and take you to your first period class."

As we pass the cafeteria, it's easy to guess what's on the menu (there's no mistaking the smell of fish sticks). I wonder if they'll serve corn and mashed potatoes with them or just French fries. Either way I really don't care. I just hope they have chocolate milk and ice-cream sandwiches. If they don't, I might be following Gram's trail of Camels all the way back to Punxsutawney.

We finally reach my locker, and Mr. Augur slips me a small piece of paper with my combination 2:2:0. I have no trouble remembering this: two sets of parents, two sets of parents who didn't want me, and no sets of parents left. Mr. Augur looks at the piece of paper and then at me and whispers, "Don't lose this or share it with anyone. If you do, the consequences could be devastating."

Since I don't want to take a chance with devastation (especially on my first day) and I already have it memorized, I consider rolling the paper into a little ball and eating it. Really, the worst thing that could happen is someone breaks in and steals my books. I can live with that. But my lunch money? Now, that would be devastating.

Mr. Augur points to a door with a sign on it that reads "Ms. Grackle's Seventh Grade English," and says, "Here's your class, River. And—I almost forgot. Here's your schedule. Good luck," he says after pulling the piece of paper from his pocket and handing it to me. Then he opens the door for me and turns to walk away.

Nineteen pairs of eyes stare at me. I consider sticking out my tongue but clench my teeth so tight there's no chance of it escaping.

Ms. Grackle smiles real big at me and acts all excited, like she'd just won a national bingo tournament or something. And I'll bet my fish sticks she hasn't a clue about the red lipstick smudged across her left front tooth.

"Well, you must be River," she says. Since I'm not carrying a neon sign, she must have seen my peel-and-stick name tag, and that makes me think I smell mothballs again.

Ms. Grackle points her long, skinny finger with bright red nail polish toward an empty desk, so I sit down. "Perfect timing," she says. "The class just finished choosing partners for our year-end project. This year is the very first year I've allowed partners. Normally students have to work all alone." Then she points to a kid in the front row. "I'm sure William's glad you're here. Now he'll have a partner just like everybody else."

Ms. Grackle hands out a detailed instruction sheet explaining what's required for our project. We must work together to decide on a topic of interest to research, complete a hands-on related project, and, finally, present it to the class. The last sentence on the sheet states, "Must include an essay" (and that, in my opinion, is the meanest word in the entire English language).

"All right, class," Ms. Grackle shouts, trying to get everyone's attention. "Don't forget that you are to do this project without the help of your parents" (she certainly has nothing to worry about with me). Then she waves her finger back and forth across the room. "And if I find out your parents helped in any way, shape, or form, you will automatically receive an F."

While Ms. Grackle rambles on, I look around the room at the other students and realize something. William didn't have a partner because no one chose him. He's the class dork. The signs are obvious. He's wearing tan pants with a crease all along the front (a dead giveaway that they were ironed by his mother this morning). And even though I realize pants creep up when you sit, it looks like he's waiting for a serious flood. His are nearly up to his knees and showing off pure white socks (which would've blended in better with sneakers). But he's wearing brown leather shoes, and neither one has a single scuff mark. He probably polishes them. His dress shirt matches his tan pants perfectly, and it's buttoned clear up to his chin. To top it off, he doesn't have a single hair out of place. Not one. But he's my partner, and there's nothing I can do about it.

I tell myself that even though he looks like a dork, there's a chance he's probably nice. Gram says, "If you judge a book by its cover, you just might miss a Hemingway."

All of a sudden, William raises his hand.

Ms. Grackle nods. "Yes, William?"

"Ms. Grackle, may a parent help due to safety factors?"

I figure the whole class will laugh, but no one does.

"Good question, William," she answers. "Of course if safety is a concern, as in your situation, parent involvement is permitted."

Just then the bell rings, and William turns toward me. "See you later, River. I'm glad we're partners."

Then everyone rushes out the door. Everyone but me. Ms. Grackle must have noticed that I have no idea where I'm supposed to go.

"River," she says, "do you know where your next class is?"

"Not exactly," I answer (which is the most polite thing I can make myself say because I'm trying hard not to say that I have no idea, and I couldn't care less because I don't even want to be here).

Ms. Grackle takes my schedule and looks it over. "You have PE. That stands for physical education, just in case you call it 'gym' where you come from." Then she points toward the hall. "Take a right and go straight to the end. You can't miss the gym."

4

A Birding Place?

I have no idea how, but I make it through PE, science, lunch, and finally math when the dismissal bell rings.

Even with mobs of students racing to their buses, William manages to find me. "Hi, River," he says. "Remember me from English?"

"Sure, I remember. I may be new, but I don't have memory issues."

William's carrying a massive stack of books in his left arm, so I think my English partner is not only a dork, but a bookworm too (which can be helpful when it comes to school projects). Then I notice his right arm is dangling at his side like a dead trout on a fishing rope, just hanging there without an ounce of life.

He looks up at me through thick, smudged lenses, using my shadow to block the sun. "Would you like to go to the library with me? We only have three weeks to get our project done, and I'd really like to get an A."

Now, hanging out at a library on a Friday afternoon isn't normally on my list of things to do, but I shrug my shoulders. "Sure, I suppose it won't hurt." I was going to help Gram unpack, but since this is for school, she'll be glad.

William leads the way along the sidewalk, and we talk about our project. Ms. Grackle said we can pick any topic as long as we follow her guidelines. I cross my fingers, wishing William wants to do something related to hockey or baseball, but I suppose I could handle something dorky like "How to Build Model Skyscrapers out of Toothpicks" (which I'd bet he's done before).

As we talk, we pass through the middle of town where there's a flower garden. And right in the center of the garden is a huge fountain, which is at least five times as tall as me. It has three different levels, and each one has carved-stone birds getting water splashed over their heads.

William walks over to the fountain. "Isn't this amazing?"

I look it over again. "Sure...as amazing as fountains can be."

"It flows all the time and never shuts off," he says, "even when Birdsong loses electricity."

"So?"

"That's because it has its own generator, believe it or not."

"Did I say I didn't believe you?"

At first William doesn't say a thing. Then he says, "Well, no. But anyways, the fountain's actually a memorial for our last mayor, Mr. Kingfisher. Everyone thought he was a great guy. One day he even saved a kid from drowning in the river. And he really loved birds. He used to have about fifty bird feeders all over his yard. Then after he died, his wife had this fountain built in his honor. She also planned on making a birding place, something else our community would enjoy, but then she ended up dying and never had the chance to build it."

"What's so special about a birding place? I've never even heard of one."

William looks at me like I'm from Mars. "Oh," he says. "Well, a birding place is very tranquil. It's filled with a variety of flowers that draw in the area birds. People go there to watch them, to be quiet and reflect, and to enjoy nature. And if they're built right, a birding place is a real thing of beauty."

"Well, a thing of beauty or not, the whole idea sounds kind of weird."

William shrugs his left shoulder. "It's really not. I probably just didn't explain it well. You know," he says, "I just had an idea. Since Mrs. Kingfisher never had the chance to make the birding place, maybe we could do that for our project."

All I can do is stare at William and wonder if he's for real.

"I actually know a great deal about birds," he says, "so it wouldn't be that difficult. And I know the perfect spot for one—right along Meadowlark River. My parents own land there.

I look straight in his eyes. "If you're telling the truth and you actually know a lot about birds and you own the land, then you've got a deal." I reach out to shake on it but quickly put my hand back in my pocket—I forgot about his dangling arm. "Anyways," I say, "it looks like this project won't be hard after all...an easy A."

"I'm not sure about that," he says, "but I do think it'll be enjoyable."

We head for the library again, but now we're quiet. Since we already talked about our project, I don't think either one of us knows what to talk about. Then all of a sudden, my mouth opens, and I start rambling about anything that pops into my head (which can happen when I feel awkward). "One time I found a baby duck sitting in a puddle, so I named her Puddles." Now William probably thinks I'm telling a joke, but I'm not. And since he doesn't laugh, I keep right on talking. "That poor little duck must have sat down and given up. She probably couldn't keep up with the rest of the ducklings on account of her crooked leg. I'm not sure if she was born like that or if she'd been hurt. She tried following me, but when I realized she couldn't walk, I picked her up and brought her home."

William nods. "Good thing you were there to save her."

"Anyways, Puddles reminded me of my Gram, since she has a crooked leg too. That's because she got sick with polio when she was a kid. She had to stay in bed for a whole year, so in three hundred and sixty-five days, she read over four hundred books. I think

I'd have died. A book's okay now and then, but four hundred's way too many."

I look at William, and he's still smiling and nodding, so I keep on talking. "Then as Puddles grew, her feet got extremely big and wide—even for a duck. Gram said they looked like two big paddles, so we changed her name to Paddles. She'd waddle around our farmhouse with a limp and her big white bottom swaying side to side. Gram has a big bottom too, and on account of her polio, she walks with a limp that makes her waddle. She calls it her 'Louisiana limp,' since that's where she lived when she got it. And Gram has a big, puffed-out chest too. I think it's because her heart's big. Her doctor says she's got an enlarged heart. It's a thing called 'cardiomegaly' or something like that. It just means she has a heart that's real big...but I don't see how having a big heart could be a bad thing."

William shrugs his left shoulder. "Me either. It seems if someone has a big heart, it would be a good thing because they'd have more love to share."

Good point, I think to myself, but kind of mushy for a boy to say.

We finally reach the library. I'm a step behind William when he tries opening the door, and for the first time, I realize how much trouble a dangling arm can be. He tries pulling the handle with a finger from his good arm, since the others are gripping his books. Then before I can help, his stack of books crashes to the ground. "Oops," he says and picks them up like it's no big deal. Now if that were me, I'd probably be yelling something that would get us kicked out of Birdsong's library before we stepped foot inside.

William picks a table beside a huge window. It's probably the best spot in the whole library, because the sun's shining in and spreading itself clear across the table, right along with William's books (which he arranges in two perfectly straight rows). He rattles off a hundred ideas he has for the birding place and starts writing them in his notebook (which is completely organized with tabs, paper, dividers, and a pouch filled with perfectly sharpened pencils).

As soon as I see his handwriting, I know I have to do something. "I think I'd better write our notes," I tell him. "They didn't teach me to read chicken scratch in Punxsutawney."

Then I'm not sure if I made William turn red or if he just got hot all of a sudden from the sun. "I know," he says. "Most of the time I can't read my writing either. My dad said I was supposed to be right handed, but because of my arm, I had to learn to be a lefty." William's glasses are halfway down his nose at this point, so he angles his head to see me. "It's not easy writing with your left hand when you're supposed to be a righty."

Now I feel smaller than a flea. "So what happened anyways?" I say, hoping I didn't hurt his feelings too bad and thinking I probably shouldn't have asked.

William must have sensed how I felt. "It's okay," he says. "I'm used to it. My arm's been like this since I was one day old."

"So you were born like that?"

"Kind of, but not exactly," he says. "My arm would have been fine, but I was born breech, which means I came out backward, feet first instead of my head. My shoulder got caught on the way out, and the nerves to my arm were stretched too far and got damaged. It's called a 'brachial plexus birth injury.'"

My stomach begins to feel queasy as I imagine William coming out of his mother backward, all tangled up on something I don't even want to think about, but William just sits there and smiles...and when I look at him, I realize his smile is a little crooked, just like mine. Then I have this thought and wonder if we could be related. Gram said people who are adopted can think like this because deep down we wonder where we came from and who we really belong to. One time I saw this happy mom and dad with a ton of kids, and I wondered if they were my real parents. It's highly possible to lose a kid when you have that many, so I thought that maybe I've just been lost all this time. So when I noticed William's crooked smile, my brain automatically thought we must be related. And no matter how many times I tell myself to stop thinking like that, it's not long before I do the same thing all over again.

William is completely unaware of what's going through my head, so he keeps explaining. "My arm's kind of like a tool without a battery. Since there's no power going to my muscles, they don't work. And I can't feel anything either. A match could touch it or I could lean against something sharp, and I wouldn't know. I have to be careful."

"That's too bad."

"Not really," he says. "It's just part of the plan. My dad's a pastor, and he says someday when I get to heaven, I'll find out why I have an arm like this. But until I get there, I've decided to do the best with what I've got."

I'm not sure what I think about all that, but I make a decision anyway. William will do our reading, and I'll write the notes. I reach for his pen and perfectly organized notebook.

Our brainstorming session grows longer and longer, and there doesn't seem to be an end to William's ideas. He says Ms. Grackle likes it when students do something out of the ordinary. Since I'm partners with William, that won't be hard to do.

I write our plan like a list:

1. Make a birding place along Meadowlark River to attract different kinds of birds.

2. Take pictures of the birds with William's camera.

3. Tape the pictures on a big piece of cardboard to display during our presentation.

4. Make labels for each kind of bird we have a picture of and include five interesting facts (William made me write the word "interesting").

5. Write an essay about our project and explain why we picked this topic, what steps we took to complete the project, and what we learned from working with a partner.

William thinks for sure we'll get an A. Bookworms are usually right about things like that.

* *

5

Ecotones

I promised to meet William at seven o'clock the next morning (which is definitely out of the ordinary for me, especially on a Saturday). I'd rather be watching cartoons and eating a bowl of Frosted Wheat Flakes with Gramp, like we used to do.

I drag my feet along the edge of Meadowlark Lane and make my way toward William's house. Carrying Gram's big bag of gardening tools makes it seem farther than it really is. We only live a quarter mile down the road from each other, which is a good thing so Gram doesn't have to drive me and use up all her gas. But even if she had to, she'd never say she minded.

I see William waiting at the side of the road, right by his mailbox. He's holding a bag of birdseed under his left arm and steadying a long metal pole with a wooden bird feeder on top. When I reach him, I can't keep myself from laughing because his hair is sticking out in every direction you can find on a compass, which is totally different than yesterday at school. And he has flower seed packages sticking out from every pocket on his pants and shirt (but somehow this doesn't surprise me). "Nice hairdo," I tell him. "Looks like you just crawled out of bed."

"I did." William smiles, and I can tell he wants to press it down, but his arm is full.

Somehow he manages to carry the metal pole with the bird feeder and the bag of birdseed in his left arm as he leads the way across the street toward the Meadowlark River. He pushes aside a few branches with his left shoulder, and I follow him along the cool, wooded trail. The ground is covered in green moss that feels like a pillow beneath my feet, and the air smells like old leaves and pine needles. After a while the trail ends in a big, flat grassy field, which looks like a green flannel blanket spread wide open and leads me right to the river.

I stand at the edge and look out. The river swirls and rushes with shades of blue I've never seen before. And it's so wide that I can't tell what's on the other side. I creep to the very edge of the bank and look over. The water's so far down I almost feel dizzy. I'm not sure which is stronger—the beauty of the river or my fear. Then it splashes against the cliff, sprays a cool mist all over my face, and makes me smile.

William says that even though his family owns the land, every-one in Birdsong comes here and walks along the river. And I can see that's true because there's a worn path stretching clear along the river in both directions.

"Why don't you put up posted signs?" I ask.

"There's no need for that. My parents believe in sharing and want everyone to feel welcome. That's just how they are. You'll see."

I check my watch. It's only seven fifteen. "So why'd we have to start so early in the morning, anyways?"

William looks surprised, as if I ought to know. "If we want to get an A on a bird project," he says, "we need to understand them. And the best way to do that is to be like a bird...and birds get up early."

Now, even though I don't know much about birds, except for the fact they fly and have feathers, I try to sound like I do. "Well, that might be true for the morning dove, but don't forget about the evening dove. We could have got together this evening and been just as much like a bird."

I think William catches on to my lack of bird knowledge because it actually looks like he's holding back a grin. "They're actually not 'morning' doves. They're mourning doves," he says. "And that's because of the sad sound they make—*wh' hooo hoo hoo hooo*—like they're sad or mourning."

I still think I have a chance of sounding smart. "Well, there's still such a thing as an evening dove, right?"

He shakes his head.

* * *

William reaches in Gram's gardening bag and pulls out her measuring tape. He looks around real slowly. "You know, River," he says, "this place is a perfect ecotone."

"An eco-what?"

"An ecotone," he says and then laughs (he's not really making fun of me—I think he just finds it funny that I don't know as many big words as he does). Then he explains. "An ecotone is an area where different habitats meet, like this area. We have a river, a sunny field, plus a wooded section...so this just happens to be the perfect spot for a birding place. Basically, it means we'll be able to attract a wide variety of birds."

But I'm afraid the only thing we're going to attract is attention (and probably too much).

While we measure our ecotone and mark it with Gram's garden stakes and string, a lady with a big, red, frizzy hairdo and a giant, bear-like dog comes by. "Hi, William." she says. "Bee-u-tee-ful morning, isn't it?" She's chomping her gum so hard I'm expecting her jaws will disconnect right in front of me. "What 'cha working on?"

William pets her bear-dog, and it starts licking him all over the place, even on his dangling arm (which sways back and forth with every lick). It must be weird to have a dog lick your arm but not be able to feel its warm, slobbery tongue against your skin.

William tells her we're making a community birding place for our school project, something Mrs. Kingfisher never got the chance to do.

"Well I'll be," she says, still chomping her gum. "That is stu-pen-dous!"

William looks toward me. "And this is my new friend, River. She just moved here from Punxsutawney, Pennsylvania. And, River," he says, "this is Mrs. Martin."

"Nice to meet you, River," she says, pulling her bear-dog away from William's arm. "Well, how about that," she says (*chomp chomp*), "I just had an epiphany. Here I am out walking along a river, and then I get to meet one." Then she laughs like she's a world famous comedian. And besides being annoyed that she's messing with my name, all I can think of is that her hairdo would make the perfect home for a family of birds.

"I'm not making fun of ya, sweetie," she says. "River's a great name. I'm just making a play on words, that's all. And by the way, we'll be seeing a lot of each other at school. I work in the cafeteria."

Now that I know she's our cafeteria lady, I'm able to forget about the name joke and the nest of birds in her hair because a cafeteria lady is a very important person to know (I plan on making sure she stocks up on chocolate milk and ice-cream sandwiches).

Then Mrs. Martin notices William's seed packages sticking out of his pockets and says, "Looks like you're gonna plant flowers to draw in the birds."

William tells her about every kind of seed we're going to plant and which birds will like which flowers. And I can't tell for sure, but I think she may be interested.

Mrs. Martin nods her head and smiles. "You know, I've got a lot of bee balm growing in my garden—some people call it

Monarda. I'll dig up a patch to share. Your seeds are gonna take a while to grow, so if you plant some of my bee balm, it'll give you and the birds some instant gratification…isn't that what we all want? Instant coffee? Instant iced tea?" And then she laughs again, which makes her frizzy, big red do bop around in the wind. "Those darlin', ruby-throated hummingbirds just love that flower, and so do the butterflies—especially the butterflies. I'll bring a clump of it to church for you tomorrow."

"Thanks, Mrs. Martin," William says.

Then Mrs. Martin takes her bear-like, licking dog and strolls away, saying, "And just wait 'til you see all the butterflies."

Okay, so now we're not only inviting a variety of birds to our birding place, but we're inviting butterflies too. This means more work—more interesting facts for our display, more photos to take, and an extra paragraph in our essay (but at least I'm guaranteed chocolate milk and ice-cream sandwiches for the rest of the school year).

* * *

After we have the ground ready with all the grass pulled out and clumps of dirt broken, William takes Gram's hoe and makes seven long, straight rows.

"Why are you making them perfectly straight?" I ask, trying not to sound too annoyed. "Don't you think we should toss the seeds all over the place so it looks more natural? You know, like a field of wildflowers?"

William shakes his head. "Order is a part of nature, so they need to be straight."

Then I say to myself so he can't hear, "If we're supposed to be acting like birds, you don't need to get all weird about it, unless you're trying to be a cuckoo bird."

* * *

As we cover the last seeds with dirt, a kid with long, greasy hair comes by. He's wearing torn jeans and a sweat-stained T-shirt. He's holding a fishing pole in one hand and a beat-up tackle box in the other. With no expression on his face, he walks over to William and grunts, "Hey."

William doesn't smile but answers, "Hey."

The kid walks around and scopes out everything. He looks at Gram's gardening tools, at the bird feeder, and at William's empty seed packs, which he pokes with his fishing pole. "What are ya doin'?" he says.

William tells him we're working on a project, but he doesn't bother to introduce me. It's not that I mind (in fact, I'm glad since that kid gives me the creeps). I just think it's weird. William introduced me to the cafeteria lady, and he seems like the type of kid who's been taught good manners.

The kid stands there and doesn't say a word. He shifts his weight back and forth, from one leg to the other, like he's nervous or something. Then he glares at William, kicks the seed packages, and walks away, heading down the river. As he leaves, I see a leather wallet sticking out of his pocket. It's hooked to a long silver chain that glistens in the sun.

William doesn't say goodbye. He just stares at the kid until he's out of sight.

I rub the goose bumps on my arms. "Who was that?"

William's gripping Gram's shovel so hard his knuckles are white. "Robert Killdeer," he says. "Just some kid who has nothing better to do than hang around here and try to intimidate me."

"Why would he do that?"

William shrugs his shoulder. "Who knows?" he says. "It's no big deal. Let's get back to work."

✶ ✶ ✶

As William digs the hole for the bird feeder, a tall man comes out from the trail and walks over to us. He puts his hand on William's shoulder. "How's everything going, Billy?" Then he looks at me and says, "And you must be River." (I check my shirt to make sure I'm not still wearing my name tag).

William says to me, "River, this is my dad. Most everyone calls him Pastor Henry."

William's dad—or maybe I should say Billy's dad—looks at me. His eyes are dark brown like a melted chocolate bar, and they match his curly brown hair. "Billy's told me all about you," he says (but there couldn't have been much to tell, except that I was late for my first day of school, that I have a grandmother who waddles like a duck, and that my handwriting is much neater than his son's). "I like your name," he says. "I've heard it only once before." Then he looks out across the water like his thoughts are somewhere else. "How did your parents decide to name you River?"

I should be used to that question by now, but each time someone asks, it feels like I'm answering for the first time. My insides get all tight and tangled up like a knotted old shoelace. "I'm not sure," I tell him, trying to think of what to say. "...I'm adopted, and that's just the name I came with. But someday I'm going to find out."

Pastor Henry nods and smiles, and when he does, I notice his smile is crooked like William's (which makes it like mine). "Well, River," he says, "I believe you will. Seek and ye shall find."

I'm not sure what I'm supposed to say to that.

Then Pastor Henry looks around—back toward the woods, across the grassy field, at the river again, and says, "This is a perfect ecotone." That's exactly what William said. Gram says an apple doesn't fall far from the tree. I think I finally get what she means.

Pastor Henry checks the work we've done and gives us each a

high-five (which is something I didn't know pastors were allowed to do). "Keep up the good work," he says, "and let me know if you need help. I'll be home preparing tomorrow's sermon." Then he heads back toward the trail, whistling.

William pushes Gram's shovel into the hole trying to make it deeper, but then he stops. "By the way," he says, "my family calls me Billy, but at school everyone calls me William. That's because there's another Billy in our grade. You can call me Billy too if you like."

"Sure. I'll call you Billy." I watch while he tries digging. "You want me to do that?" I say. "Using a shovel with only one hand looks pretty hard."

"That's okay," he says. "I've got it." He digs a few more scoops of dirt and then stops to measure. "Deep enough," he says. "If I hold the pole in there real straight, can you pack dirt around it?"

"I'll try." When it's as packed as I can get it, Billy wiggles the pole. At first it moves just a little. Then it leans like the Tower of Pisa.

"Well," he says, "we should've used cement, but we can find rocks and pile them around the base. That'll help tighten it."

"Are you serious? We have to hunt for rocks?"

"If you want to get an A."

6

Rock Hunters

We head to the trail and search the woods for rocks. I go one way and Billy goes the other. I walk around pine trees while searching the ground, when all of a sudden, I find a gold mine. "Hey, Billy," I shout. "There's a huge pile of rocks over here."

"That's great, River. I found some flat ones here," he shouts back. "They'll be good for stacking. Let me bring mine to the trail, and I'll be right over."

I look through the pile, finding all the flat ones and stacking them off to the side when I hear a noise. "Hey, Billy! Do you hear that?"

"Hear what?"

"That noise."

"I don't hear anything over here."

"Well, hurry up and get over here. It sounds pretty cool...like a maraca or a baby's rattle."

"A what?"

"Never mind," I say. "It's probably a weird West Virginia locust or something." I pick through the pile for more flat rocks. The noise gets louder.

Billy shouts from the far side of the trail. "Did you say rattle?"

"Ah, yeah, like ten light years ago."

"I'm coming, River! Stand completely still," he shouts. "Don't move!"

"Cut it out, Billy," I yell back. "Do you really think I feel like playing a stupid game like statues?"

Billy stops running when he's a few feet away, and then he moves toward me in slow motion. "River," he whispers, "you have to trust me. Don't move a muscle."

I freeze and whisper back. "There. I'm frozen…stiffer than a granite angel on a tombstone. Are you happy? Now, will you please tell me what you think about this noise?"

Billy puts his finger to his lips and says, "Shhh…" Then he searches the area with his eyes, which stop dead at the edge of the rock pile, inches from where I am. I follow where his gaze stops. Coiled beside my pile of flat rocks is what's making the noise. And although I've never seen one in real life, I know exactly what a rattlesnake is when I see it. I couldn't move if I wanted to. My legs are so weak I can hardly stand. I want to scream but I know I can't.

Billy reaches toward me real slow, and then he takes my hand and whispers, "We're going to step backward very slowly, River. Like this…"

I copy Billy and take one slow step backward and then another and another, each one without a sound. Not even a stick cracks beneath our feet. We walk backward until we reach the trail when Billy lets go of my hand. "Wow, River," he says. "Someone from upstairs was looking out for you."

I look at him, wondering what he means.

He points to the sky. "You know, upstairs? As in heaven?"

"What does heaven have to do with rattlesnakes?"

"Well," he says, "I'm pretty sure God was looking out for you."

"You think so?"

"Sure! How else can you explain it? Do you have any idea how close that was? I can't believe it didn't strike you."

"Well, maybe it's not the kind that bites."

"Oh, it is. And it definitely felt threatened. That's why it was rattling. Anyways, let's not get any more rocks from piles. This time we're staying on the trail."

I shake my head. "There's no way I'm looking for more rocks."

"Don't worry," he says. "I'll find them."

"I guess that was pretty close, wasn't it?"

"It definitely was. But whatever you do," Billy says, "don't tell my parents, or they might not let us finish our project."

"Well, maybe we shouldn't. We could always do something different."

Billy shakes his head. "Not a chance. We'll be fine as long as we stay away from that rock pile."

* * *

By twelve o'clock we finished almost everything on our list. Plus we even rolled a log over to the end of the trail, right where it meets the field. Billy says people can sit on it while they're bird watching (which doesn't sound that exciting, if you ask me). "Do you really think anyone's going to come, or even stay long enough to sit down? Besides, do people even want to watch birds?"

Billy sits on the log and then turns to look at me. "You need to be patient, River. Just wait until you see how interesting birds are. I think you'll be surprised."

I brush a clump of dirt off the log and sit beside him. "How can you be so sure birds will even come? I bet we don't see any."

Billy reaches out his left hand. "Bet you a tall glass of lemonade that by the time we're done building this birding place, there'll be more birds than you can imagine. Sparrows, bluebirds, mourning doves, chickadees..."

I shake with my left hand too. "Well, if I were you," I say, "I wouldn't go betting on something like birds because you're gonna be awful thirsty while I'm sipping a tall, cold glass of lemonade."

Billy smiles his crooked smile. "We'll see."

7

The Meeting of the Whippoorwills

The last thing on our list is to make a birdbath (and with all the water in the Meadowlark River, I'm not sure why we need one). But for some reason, Billy thinks the birds need even more. And then, believe it or not, Billy tells me he's come up with a new list of things we need to do, but I haven't seen it because he has it stored in his head (plus, I'm not sure I want to know what's on it because it's probably going to mean more work).

Billy checks his watch. "This is a perfect time for a break. Want to come to my house for lunch? I already asked my mom if you could, and she said yes."

So that's what I say too.

★ ★ ★

When we walk into Billy's house, I can't believe my eyes. There are kids all over the place, and each one looks like they're having a blast. They're jumping on the couch, climbing on the chairs, crawling under the rug, and sliding down the stairs, and one's standing right in the middle of the kitchen table (with his shoes on).

"Forrest," his mother says, smiling while she scoops him up, "get off the table. Even though you're little, you know the rules."

Now, right away I know she's not like Gram because Gram would let Paddles climb up on the table every morning and eat breakfast with us. I'd give her a bowl of Frosted Wheat Flakes since that's what she liked best, but Gram would feed her plain old grits, oatmeal, or a piece of cornbread. She said all those sugared flakes made Paddles flap around the house like a chicken with her head cut off (and I know Paddles didn't appreciate that comment one bit).

Billy introduces me to his mother and all the kids. But there's no way I'll remember their names since there's six of them. And I'm not sure what to call Billy's mom because he actually forgot that part, but I figure if his dad is Pastor Henry, she must be Mrs. Henry.

Pastor Henry gathers all the kids, using his hands like a broom to sweep up a bunch of wild dust bunnies. Then he picks up Forest and sets him in a high chair while Mrs. Henry pulls out a chair for me.

"Thanks, Mrs. Henry," I say, trying to be sure I use every bit of manners I know.

Mrs. Henry's real pretty, and when she smiles, her blue eyes sparkle. "Most people call me Mrs. Whippoorwill," she says, "since that's our last name. Billy's dad is called Pastor Henry because Henry is his first name, and it's easier for people to call him Pastor Henry than Pastor Whippoorwill." She smiles at me again and says, "I know that's confusing, River." Mrs. Whippoorwill tries real hard so I don't feel as dumb as I do.

While Mrs. Whippoorwill passes out the plates and silverware, I start worrying that Billy's going to say something about the *morning* and *evening* dove thing. If he does, I might have to slide under the table and vanish.

In the center of the table, Mrs. Whippoorwill sets a gigantic pot that's overflowing with macaroni and cheese with little pieces of hot dog. She plops a supersized scoop of it in the middle of everyone's plate (which must be the easiest way to serve food when there's a gazillion mouths to feed). I don't particularly like my food all mixed together like that, but I keep my mouth shut and resist the urge to separate my noodles from the bits of hot dog. Right before I start to dig in, I suddenly realize everyone's holding everyone else's hands and putting their heads down (not all the way down on the table, like you do at school when you're in trouble, but just partway down), like they're looking for a piece of hot dog they dropped on their lap.

Then Pastor Henry says, "Dear heavenly Father, we give thanks for our food and for all our blessings. Thank you for Billy's new friend, River. Help us live our lives pleasing to you. Amen."

Then everybody else, including little Forrest, shouts, "Amen!"

By now, I figure I'm officially known by everyone in Birdsong as Billy's new friend (and added to that just seconds ago, as the girl who doesn't know people in Birdsong hold hands and pray before they eat).

$$\ast\ \ast\ \ast$$

After lunch me and Billy go back across the street to the birding place. He carries the garbage can lid we'll use to make the birdbath. "So," he says, "what do you think of my last name?"

"It sure is different. I've never heard the name Whippoorwill before."

Billy stops on the trail, and his eyes grow bigger than fifty-cent pieces. "You've never heard of a whip-poor-will?"

I shake my head and start feeling dumb all over again.

"That's okay," he says and starts walking. "It's just a name—like the whip-poor-will bird. They blend in with tree bark and dead leaves on the ground, so they can be real hard to see. But even though you can't always see them, you'll know they're there."

"Okay, Mr. Know-it-all," I tease, "how do you know they're there if you can't see them?"

"Because you hear them...especially on summer evenings. They sound like they're saying *whip-poor-will, whip-poor-will, whip-poor-will.*"

"Wow! That's kind of neat." I'm beginning to think Billy may be right—birds are more interesting than I thought.

We reach the birding place, and Billy sets the lid beside the pole with the wooden bird feeder. "I'm glad we had a plastic lid. Metal would get too hot in the sun," he says. "Now all we have to do is build a base to keep the birdbath just high enough off the ground to keep stray cats or a fox from catching the birds. The base will be easy to make. We can use rocks again. And we should put a couple inside the lid so it doesn't blow away."

"You know, Billy, do you think the birds even need a birdbath? There's a ton of water right here in the river. Besides, I didn't think this was going to be so much work. And I definitely don't want to look for rocks again."

Billy spreads the dirt flat where we'll put the birdbath. "First of all," he says, "yes, the birds need a birdbath. Even though some of the bigger birds, like ducks and blue herons, love the river, it's too big and dangerous for some of the smaller birds that like to drink and bathe in a small, safe place. And second," he adds, "getting an A is hard work. But don't worry about the rocks. I'll find them."

8

Another List

We've been working since seven o'clock this morning (with only a half-hour lunch break), so I've been hoping Billy would forget about the new list of things he wants to do. But, of course, he doesn't (bookworms are like elephants—they never forget).

He tells me what's on his list like he's reading from an encyclopedia. "First we need to scatter small pieces of yarn and cloth throughout our ecotone. Birds will use them to make nests. Second, we'll make suet, which is a type of bird food. And third, we need to build several bluebird houses."

"Are you serious?" I say. "With all this work, we'd better get an A plus, not just an A."

As Billy sets the last rock on top of the birdbath, I start wondering how we're going to fill it. I think about all the water we're going to need to water our seeds and fill the birdbath. Then I think about how steep and high the riverbank is. The Meadowlark River rushes fast, so it could be dangerous to get water from there. I look at Billy and say, "Are we carrying water all the way from your house?"

"We could," he says, "but I'm sure there's a way to get it from the river. It would be a lot less work, that's for sure."

Since I like to work as little as possible, my brain starts spinning ideas faster than a gerbil spins an exercise wheel. "What if we tied a long rope to a bucket and dropped it over the edge of the riverbank? We could pull up the bucket, like pulling up a bucket of water from a well."

Billy smiles (he's probably thinking I'm pretty smart too). "Great idea!" he says. "Let's run back to my garage and get everything we'll need."

Walking into Billy's garage is like walking into an inventor's museum. It's filled with all sorts of old interesting metal and wooden things. There are piles of wood, cans of paint stacked on shelves, hammers and screwdrivers hanging on the wall, and rows of glass baby-food jars filled with nails. Billy reaches for a hammer and says, "This is my dad's workshop. We build things together all the time."

I can't even imagine how awesome that would be. "You're so lucky, Billy." I run my hands across his wooden workbench. "When my parents find me, I'm going to build things with my dad too."

All of a sudden Billy stops rummaging around. "What do you mean, when your parents find you? I thought you said you were adopted. Don't you have parents?"

"I have two," I say. "Two sets, so I actually have four parents. I just don't live with them. I live with Gram—she's my grandmother." Billy looks at me like I'm not making sense, so I explain. "I have my real parents, and then I have my adoptive parents. That makes four."

"I understand why you don't live with your real parents, but why don't you live with your adoptive parents?"

"Well, it's sort of a mixed-up story," I say, but I decide to tell him anyway. "For some reason, after my adoptive parents had me for six months, they decided they didn't want me anymore. That's when they took off and left me behind. They never came back. Now I live with Gram."

"So which parents do you want to find you?"

"My real ones, because I figure they never wanted to give me up in the first place...I'm sure they must have had a good reason. But I guess it would be all right if my adoptive parents come back because they'd probably have information about my real ones."

"Did you ever try finding your real parents?"

"No," I say and look at him. "I told you I didn't come with much information. All I know is my first name and the birth-date that was on my necklace, which isn't much information to go on. And Gram doesn't know anything either. But I'm not worried about it, because I'm sure my real parents have been looking for me. So by this time they should be getting close. They could show up here any time now."

"Well, after we finish our project, I'll help you with some research."

"Maybe," I tell him.

Billy looks surprised. "What do you mean, maybe? Don't you think that would be a good idea? Birdsong's an extremely small town, so I doubt they'll look for you here." Billy searches my eyes. "River, maybe you should start looking for them."

"I told you I don't have to worry about that. Gram says the post-master knows our new address, so when they get to Punxsutawney, they'll know where to come."

Billy looks at me the same way Gram does when I talk about my parents finding me—like he doesn't believe it will happen either. Billy shrugs his shoulder and then pulls a rusted red wagon out from the corner of the garage. He brushes it off. "Anyways," he says, "let's use this to haul our supplies." Then he finds a rope, an old metal bucket, two green sprinkling cans, and a small, square wire thing hanging from a hook. It looks a bit like an animal cage, but it'd be too small, even for a gerbil. Billy smiles and holds it up like it's a trophy.

"What in the world is that?"

"This is a suet cage," he says, "a special type of bird feeder. Now, when we make suet cakes, we'll have a way to hang them. Woodpeckers, chickadees, and nuthatches love suet. And," he adds, "so does my favorite bird."

"Which is what kind?" I figure I might as well ask because he's going to tell me anyway.

"The bluebird," he says as he smiles. "They're incredible. And not just because of their brilliant blue feathers and how beautifully they sing, but because their mating rituals are fascinating. Imagine this. When two bluebirds are courting, which is kind of like dating, the male bluebird raises and quivers one wing while he feeds his mate little morsels of food."

"Hmmm," I say, "that is fascinating" (but even so, I'm not sure that's my idea of romance). But one thing's for sure—if Billy were a bird, he'd probably have only one wing that worked, so he'd do just fine as a bluebird. The only problem is that even though he could court, he wouldn't be able to fly...and that could be a real turnoff to a girl bird.

$$* \ * \ *$$

As we're leaving the garage, something else catches Billy's eye. He reaches up and grabs it off the shelf. "Awesome!" he says. "I knew we had one somewhere!"

"What is it?" After suet cages and suet cakes, I'm not even going to guess.

"It's a hummingbird feeder! Now we can make hummingbird nectar too!"

I don't know any other guy who knows how to make suet cakes and hummingbird nectar and gets excited about it. Gram would say, "He's a rare bird, and like a T-bone steak, sometimes rare is good."

9

The Bucket

After the wagon's loaded with our supplies, we race each other to Billy's kitchen. Mrs. Whippoorwill's standing at the sink peeling a tractor load of vegetables. Forrest and two other little Whippoorwills are racing around the kitchen with wooden cars, and the bigger ones are washing vegetables.

"Hey, Mom," Billy says, "do you have some yarn or cloth we can use for our project?"

Mrs. Whippoorwill tucks a strand of hair behind her ear. "I'm sure I can find some of each, Billy. What do you need it for?"

"We want to scatter pieces of it around our ecotone so the birds can make nests with it."

"That's a great idea," she says. "I have some blue and yellow yarn left from knitting Forrest's baby blanket and also scraps of green material from the curtains I made. That should make some colorful nests. And how about these vegetable peelings?" she says. "Do you think the birds would eat them?"

Billy shakes his head. "They'd only draw predators, and probably the kind that would eat birds."

I look at Billy. "You mean predators, like rattlesnakes?"

Billy swings around to face me, and his eyes nearly pop out of his head. He mouths the words, "What are you doing?" Then he answers out loud so his mom can hear, "Well, sure, vegetable peelings could attract snakes, so we better not take any. But the yarn and material would be great."

Billy seems pretty excited about the nest material, but I'm not sure the birds will use it. Then I imagine Billy as a bluebird and think about how he'd build his nest. He'd definitely use the blue yarn. He'd have to make sure his nest perfectly matched his brilliant, blue feathers.

Then Billy moves closer to his mom, leans on the sink, and looks at her with puppy-dog eyes. "And is it okay if we make hummingbird nectar and suet cakes too?"

Mrs. Whippoorwill smiles. "Sure, Billy. Just make me a list. There's paper and a pencil near the phone."

Billy hands them to me and tells me what to write (I'll bet his mom can't read chicken scratch either). He says, "We'll need sugar, suet, oatmeal, yellow cornmeal, flour, and crunchy peanut butter." Then he puts the list by his mom's purse.

$$* * *$$

We head back to the birding place. As Billy pulls the wagon, one of the rusty wheels cries out *screek, screek, screek*. Billy laughs. "That sounds like a bird that's having a real rotten day. Like maybe he was fighting with his brothers and sisters, and they pushed him out of the nest."

Now he's got me laughing. "Or maybe he sounds like that because he stuffed too many worms in his mouth."

"Or maybe that's what a bird sounds like when they're learning to talk. 'Mama! Dada!'"

"Whatever," I say and kick a stone off the trail.

"Sorry, River. I didn't mean to make you think about your parents."

"That's okay. It's not your fault. I think about them all the time, anyways."

When we reach our ecotone, we throw pieces of blue and yellow yarn and scraps of green material all over the place, tossing them into the wind like confetti. Some land on the branches of shrubs and trees, some near the edge of the woods, and some fall on the ground near the bird feeders and birdbath. Who knows? Maybe every bird in Birdsong will come and build a beautiful nest. I hope they do because Billy would really like that (and I think I would too).

$$* * *$$

Since we're ready for water, I get the rope and tie it to the bucket. I use a bowline knot that Gramp taught me. I remember him guiding my hands over the rope, saying, "The rabbit hops out of the hole, goes around the tree, and back down the hole." It still works like magic.

"Time to try it out," I tell Billy, "but I'm going first" (I'm not trying to be bossy—I just think it's too dangerous for Billy, and it's scary enough standing at the edge of the river with two good arms, so it could be twice as scary with only one).

I stand at the edge, dig my toes into the ground, and throw the bucket as hard and as far out into the river as I can. Then I watch it drop. It lands close to where I wanted and sinks deep into the water. I pull it up, one hand over the other, all along the length of the rope. When it reaches the top, I bend down, steadying myself with one hand, and grab the bucket with my other. But since it bumped against the cliff on the way up, it's barely half full. "Maybe we should get the water from your house," I say. "This is trickier than I thought."

Billy shakes his head. "The river's a natural resource. It's not chlorinated like tap water. The birds and flowers will thrive if they have it," he says. "We need the river water."

"Well, the bucket idea isn't working that great. Besides, don't you think it's dangerous?"

"Not if we're careful."

"Okay," I tell him, "but I get the water, and you do the watering."

Billy glares at me. "You're afraid I can't do it, aren't you?"

"No," I say feeling a little guilty for lying. "It's just that—"

"I know," he says, "it's just that I only have one arm that works, right?" He reaches for the bucket. "Give it here, River." I want to tie a rope to his belt loop in case he falls, but mostly I want to tell him not to do it.

He tucks the free end of the rope under his right foot and shifts his weight to secure it. Then he grabs the bucket in his left hand and throws it. But the wind has picked up and blows against us, so the bucket bangs against the cliff and gets caught on a root. He yanks it free and tries again. This time it goes a little farther and lands at the base of the cliff where the boulders are. Billy looks at me. "I'm not giving up," he says. "I can do this." He throws it again, and after reaching the water, it sinks fast. He pulls the rope and draws it closer. After each pull, he secures the rope under his foot. He does it over and over until it reaches the top. Then he kneels on his left knee, grabs the bucket, and brings it up over the edge. "See?"

I look inside. It's more than half full. "Wow, you did it."

He carries the bucket to the birdbath and sprinkling cans and fills them. Then when we're watering our seeds, Pastor Henry comes back to check our progress. "You chose an excellent idea for your project," he says. "I think it's wonderful to make something for our community, and I'm sure Mrs. Kingfisher would have been pleased."

All of a sudden, Pastor Henry looks at the rope and bucket. "Is that how you're getting water?"

Billy nods. I don't say a word.

"The riverbank is too steep, Billy. I'd rather you use the wagon to transport water from the house. Understand?"

Billy looks like he's about to say something, probably about the river being a natural resource, but an older couple strolls over to us before he says a word.

"Hello, Pastor Henry and Billy," the older man says, and his wife smiles like she'd said it too. He reaches out and shakes my hand. "I'm Mr. Bunting, and this is my lovely wife."

"My name is River. I'm Billy's new friend."

Billy tells them every detail about our project.

"What splendid news," says Mr. Bunting. "A perfect way to honor the Kingfishers."

Mrs. Bunting nods her head. "Perfect indeed. You know, I have plenty of pink and purple Carolina phlox in my garden that's already blooming. I'll dig up a patch to share. You'll be happy to know the hummingbirds and butterflies absolutely adore it." Then Mr. and Mrs. Bunting say the same thing, "See you at church tomorrow." With that they head down the river path, holding hands.

Pastor Henry turns to look at me. "Speaking of church, would you like to join us tomorrow morning? Service starts at eleven o'clock, but everyone comes a bit early to visit."

I'm not exactly sure what to say. "Ummm…Gram and I don't go to church, but she used to. We do chores on Sundays. And she just spent a lot of money on gas moving here, so she doesn't plan on driving for a while."

Pastor Henry keeps looking at me (he probably thinks I'm making up excuses, but I'm not). "I understand," he says, "but we keep our service short because we believe in spending time with family on Sundays too. And we'd be happy to give you and your grandmother a ride. We could pick you up just before ten thirty." Pastor Henry puts his strong hand on my shoulder and says, "I'd be happy if you'd pass the invitation on to your grandmother."

I tell him I will (even though there's no chance we'll be going).

10

Gram Accepts

*g*ram's bag of tools seems heavier as I carry it back home. And the walk feels longer too. When I finally get there, it's supper time, and Gram's pulling a steamy tuna-noodle casserole out of the oven. She's wearing her old apron with purple violets all over it, so even though it's not our kitchen back in Punxsutawney, it almost feels like it is.

"My goodness, Sugar Pie, you've been at that river the whole livelong day. Must be some project you're working on." Gram sets the casserole on the table with a clunk. "I thought I'd be eating alone. Now, wash those hands and sit down to have a bite with your old gram." Then she plops a giant scoop of tuna noodle right in the middle of my plate (maybe Mrs. Whippoorwill is a little like Gram, after all).

I tell Gram all about our birding place, about the Kingfishers, Billy's seed packages, our ecotone, the suet cakes and hummingbird nectar, the gazillion little Whippoorwills, Pastor Henry's workshop, Mrs. Martin and her licking dog, Mrs. Bunting's Carolina phlox, and about Robert—the kid with long, greasy hair who tried to intimidate Billy.

"Well, that's all wonderful, Sugar Pie, but I don't like the sounds of that Robert. I gotta think a kid who tries picking on a nice boy like Billy doesn't have both oars in the water." Gram puts a heaping spoonful in her mouth and swallows. "Well, I can hardly wait to see that birding place. How about we walk there after chores tomorrow?"

"It's about a quarter mile, Gram, so it's too far with your leg. We'd better drive."

"We're walking, Sugar Pie." Then she gives me a wink. "My physical therapist says walking will make it stronger."

I swallow my tuna noodle in one big gulp and almost drop my milk. "What? You went already?"

"I wasn't gonna start 'til we were all settled in, but this morning I heard the wind. It told me to take a drive through town, and wouldn't you know—I end up seeing a sign that said, 'Birdsong Physical Therapy Welcomes You.' So I parked Tilly on the side of the road and went right in. Come to find out, someone had just cancelled an appointment, so I grabbed it faster than a dog will lick a dish. And let me tell you, that therapist knows what he's talking about. He's no nincompoop, that's for sure. He showed me all sorts of exercises that'll make my leg strong. So tomorrow, Sugar Pie, we're walking to that birding place."

I smile at Gram. "I can't wait to show you." Then I remember Pastor Henry's invitation (even though she'll say no). "Billy's dad invited us to his church tomorrow. He's the pastor, so everyone calls him Pastor Henry. He said he'd give us a ride."

"Well, that's a nice invitation, Sugar Pie. You tell him we'll go."

I can't think of any other explanation for Gram saying yes, so I start worrying about aliens again.

* * *

After dinner I clear the table, and Gram washes, just like we did in Punxsutawney. Then before I know it, Gram looks like she's in ballet class and starts to relevé right in front of our kitchen sink while she's washing the tuna-noodle casserole dish. She raises up high on her toes, then goes down flat, up high again, then down, and all the while she's smiling like a delicate ballerina. There's just one problem. She's not. I'm pretty sure her physical therapist must have something to do with this (I just hope she doesn't start wearing a tutu).

11

* *

The Worrying Thing

At exactly ten twenty-five Sunday morning, the Whippoor-wills' big white van (which is the size of a bus) pulls in our driveway. Gram and I hurry out the door (well, I hurry and Gram waddles).

Pastor Henry rolls down his window to greet us, so I introduce Gram. "Gram, this is Pastor Henry. Pastor Henry, this is my grandmother, Mrs. Nuthatch." And to her surprise, I do it so eloquently that she freezes, speechless (and Gram is never speechless). Then she shakes her head and whispers, "Well, I'll be!"

Next thing I know, Billy jumps out, opens the van door for us, and pulls it shut once we're in (the whole while his right arm is swinging back and forth like a pendulum). I forgot to tell Gram about his arm. I wonder if she noticed.

As Gram and I squish together in the second row of seats, we're instantly surrounded by a flock of little Whippoorwills. Every one of them wants to sit on Gram's lap, and she makes sure each one does (I bet Mrs. Whippoorwill already likes Gram).

* * *

Pastor Henry's church feels real comfortable, like a bathtub filled with warm sudsy water. And no one's dressed up fancy. Most of the men are wearing jeans, and hardly any of the ladies are

wearing dresses. But Gram and Mrs. Whippoorwill are. I'm wearing a skirt (only because Gram made me). It used to be a maxi and
reached all the way to my toes. But since I've had it for three years
or more, it's directly at my knees. I hate wearing it, but Gram says
I'm a young lady now and need to start looking like one. The only
good thing about this skirt is that it's made of denim (which is as
close to a pair of jeans as Gram would let me get).

Everybody must know everybody in Pastor Henry's church
because everybody's giving hugs to everybody else. All the little
kids are running around playing and hiding from each other, and
the older ones are huddled in a group talking. Billy and I decide
to sit with the grown-ups. Mrs. Whippoorwill pours Gram a cup
of coffee, and then Gram lets me drink some just like she does at
home.

Pastor Henry's church smells delicious because at the same
table that has the coffeepot, there are seven very big boxes of
donuts. There are all kinds—cream-filled, jelly-filled, cinnamon
swirls, glazed, sugar-coated, and fried cakes (which are my favorite). And hanging right above that table is a huge picture of Jesus
standing all by himself, wearing a pair of sandals and a long, white
thing that looks something like a bathrobe (but not exactly). He's
holding his arms stretched out wide in front of him, so it actually
looks like he's guarding the donuts. Maybe Pastor Henry hung the
picture there on purpose so no one takes more than they should,
which is pretty smart. I don't think anyone would have the guts to
take more donuts than they should if Jesus is watching. I decide to
take one fried cake covered with chocolate frosting and rainbow
sprinkles (I hope that's okay with Jesus).

Gram and I are meeting everyone in Birdsong this morning
because Billy says this is what everyone in Birdsong does on Sunday mornings. They come to hang with Pastor Henry and have
free coffee and donuts.

Pretty soon the piano lady begins playing, and everyone moseys into the big part of the church, where there are beautiful stained glass windows. One of them is boarded up. Billy said someone threw a rock through it (which means Birdsong has at least one bad person). All of a sudden, I imagine Robert Killdeer holding his fishing pole in one hand, and instead of his beat-up tackle box in the other, he's gripping a rock. I never met anyone who gave me the creeps like he does.

Gram and I sit beside all the Whippoorwills, except for Pastor Henry, of course. He gets to stand on the stage so everyone can see him. I wonder if God can see him too.

The benches we're sitting on are in rows, and they're made of wood. But at least they have red velvety cushions on them. But they're not very thick, so you actually sink down to the wood. When I sneak a peek at Gram, she's grinning ear to ear, looking more comfortable than ever (I guess having a big bottom like Paddles can come in handy).

Once everybody finds a spot to sit, Pastor Henry says a prayer. "This morning, Lord, we want everything to be for you. Let our thoughts, our songs, our church, and our community be all for you. Bless our time together with your holy presence. Amen." Then he asks everyone to stand and turn to page one hundred thirty seven in our hymnal (I figure that's the blue book hanging on the back of the bench in front of me because everyone else is reaching for their blue book too).

The piano lady begins a song called "It Is Well with My Soul." Everyone joins in, even Gram. I just listen because I've never heard this song on the radio before, and I can't read music any more than I can read chicken scratch.

Then out of the blue, I start thinking about Gram's physical therapist, so I cross my fingers and make a wish that she doesn't start to relevé right in the middle of church while everyone's singing about their wellness and their soul. But I must have crossed them too late, because by the second verse she's up on her toes. "Really, Gram?" I whisper (probably a little too loud for being in church).

Then Gram whispers back (even louder), "Don't you worry, Sugar Pie. Nobody's gonna notice." So I try not to and close my eyes to concentrate on the words while everyone sings them. I try to figure out what they mean. "When peace like a river attendeth my way. When sorrows like sea billows roll. Whatever my lot, Thou hast taught me to say, 'It is well, it is well, with my soul.'" Then I'm not exactly sure when it happened, but the song ended.

Pastor Henry begins his lecture. "This morning I want to share some key points from the book of Matthew, where Jesus talks to us about worrying. He tells us not to worry about our life. Wow! Isn't that a challenge? He tells us not to worry about the food we'll eat, what we'll drink, or the clothes we'll wear. He tells us to consider the birds, to think about how they live. They don't bother storing food for themselves because they know our heavenly Father feeds them. God provides them with food and shelter. God created birds. And he takes care of them. And since we are worth more than birds, we can be sure our heavenly Father will take care of us. Jesus also makes it clear that we cannot add a single moment to our lives by worrying, so there is no sense in fretting. Therefore," Pastor Henry tells everyone, "don't worry! Our heavenly Father knows everything we need."

It sounds like Pastor Henry must like birds as much as Billy. And after hearing what Pastor Henry just read, it sounds like God probably likes birds too (he must since he goes around feeding them). And about the worrying thing, maybe I didn't need to worry about Billy falling over the edge and into the river because it sounds like no one can make anyone's life longer by worrying. Not even by a moment. I had no idea going to church could make you think so much.

When church is over, Pastor Henry stands at the door and

says goodbye to every single person and shakes their hand. He even knows everyone's name. While he's busy saying goodbye, Gram and I help Mrs. Whippoorwill and Billy clean up. We vacuum donut crumbs, wipe coffee spills, push in chairs, and then straighten all the blue songbooks (which takes quite a while because Billy says they have to be perfectly straight).

* * *

As soon as Pastor Henry brings me and Gram home, we get right to work on our chores. They actually haven't changed much from the ones we did back in Punxsutawney, except that I don't have to sweep down thirteen stairs anymore. That's because now we live in a one-story house. And now we have only one bathroom to clean (which most people would be grateful for). But honestly I'd rather clean two than have to wait all day for Gram to come out of the one we do have. Some days I think she's fallen in and accidently flushed herself away (every now and then, I go and check to make sure she hasn't).

* * *

After our chores are done, Gram and I head to the birding place. We start out walking at a pretty good pace (considering Gram's leg), when all of a sudden, she lets out a "Yee haw!" and charges down the road.

I shout ahead, "Gram, what are you doing?"

She keeps galloping full speed, then yells back over her shoulder, "Just doing my exercises, Sugar Pie!" I remember Gram saying her physical therapist knows what he's talking about, but I'm beginning to wonder. I run ahead and catch up to her when she stops galloping and begins to hop. She hops down the middle of the road the rest of the way, which is just as embarassing as her galloping.

When we finally reach the trail, I look across the street at the Whippoorwills' house and hope no one's watching from their front window. But that's not likely because with Pastor Henry, Mrs. Whippoorwill, Billy, and all six little Whippoorwills, there's eighteen eyeballs altogether. I can only hope the entire family is sitting around the kitchen table praying with their eyes closed.

Once we're in the woods, Gram stops hopping and slows to a snail's pace. She's huffing and puffing so hard I hope she doesn't have a heart attack right before she gets to see the birding place. But since her heart is extra big, I guess it can handle stuff like this.

We walk along the wooded trail, and then I let Gram step out into the field first. She stands still, looks around, then takes a deep breath in, and smiles (she looks as happy as she does after she's eaten a dozen chocolate-chip cookies dunked in milk).

Gram keeps smiling as she looks across our ecotone. All of a sudden, her eyes stop short, and she points to the bucket and rope (I wonder if all grown-ups have something against a bucket with a rope tied to it). Gram walks over to it and looks at the riverbank and then back at me. "You've been getting water with this?"

I try to remember the words Billy used..."The river's a natural resource, Gram. It's not chlorinated like tap water, and the birds and flowers need it to thrive."

Gram's jaw drops (she's probably impressed with how smart I've gotten). "That's all well and good, Sugar Pie, but this bank is too blasted steep. I wouldn't want to see anyone fall off the edge...cuz if they did, they'd never see the light of day."

"Don't worry, Gram. Remember what Pastor Henry said this morning? We can't make anyone's life longer by worrying."

"Sugar Pie, there's a difference between worrying and using your noggin."

12

Suet Cakes

The next morning I oversleep and miss the bus, so Gram drives me to school. At least I make it in time to hear the morning announcements and menu—spaghetti with meatballs for lunch. I check my schedule and realize I don't have English today. For the first time in my life, I actually wish I did.

* * *

Later at lunch, Billy spots me in the cafeteria and hurries over. "Hey, River, I'm glad I found you." He sits across the table from me. "Want to come to my house after school? My mom went shopping and bought our ingredients, so now we can make suet cakes and hummingbird nectar."

Since my mouth is filled with spaghetti, I nod. Then I don't know how he does it, but Billy opens his milk carton with one hand. When I think he's not looking, I try opening mine one-handed but end up spilling chocolate milk all over my spaghetti, myself, the table, and the floor. Two seconds later the overhead speakers blare, "Maintenance to the cafeteria. Maintenance to the cafeteria."

Billy grins and shakes his head. "Nice try, but it takes years of practice."

I shrink to the size of a meatball and want to roll out the door.

* * *

After school we hurry to Billy's house. When we get there, it's totally quiet and looks like no one's home. Mrs. Whippoorwill has everything we need for making suet cakes and hummingbird nectar sitting on the kitchen table. There's also a plate of chocolate-chip cookies.

In all of the quietness, I hear Mrs. Whippoorwill tiptoe down the stairs. She comes around the corner looking like she's just completed a marathon while carrying all her little Whippoorwills. "I just put the last one down for a nap," she says. Even though she looks like she doesn't have an ounce of energy left, she smiles at me, and her blue eyes sparkle. "It's nice you could come over, River." She makes me feel warm all over, as if the sun is shining only on me. She places her hand gently on my shoulder and says, "You're always welcome here." Then she takes a cookie from the plate and excuses herself. "Let me know if you need my help. I'll be on the couch taking a quick nap."

I guess it's just me and Billy cooking for the birds. I hope he knows what he's doing because I sure don't. Last year in Punxsutawney, I flunked home economics. Gram couldn't believe it. Neither could I. Apparently Mrs. Hawk didn't like the way my banana bread turned out (no one told me I had to peel the bananas). So what if it was like chewing an eraser. I still don't think that was grounds for failure. But then again, there was also the sewing project I messed up when I had to make a skirt. I didn't think it was a big deal that I sewed the wrong sides of the material together, but obviously Mrs. Hawk did. I tried explaining that I'd never wear the stupid skirt anyways, but that only got me an F.

Billy arranges our ingredients in alphabetical order: cornmeal, flour, oatmeal, peanut butter, and suet (he's way too enthusiastic). "Let's make suet cakes first," he says. "Step number one, we need to melt the suet." He turns the stove on and hands me a spoon. "Here, you can stir first."

I move the chunk of hard, white suet around in the pan. Within minutes it starts melting, transforming into a crystal clear liquid. I wonder if this is how it feels to be a scientist. Then all of a sudden, I realize I have no idea what suet is or where it comes from, but since it looks interesting, I stick my finger in for a taste test (just like Gram would do). But before my finger reaches my lips, Billy stops me. "I wouldn't do that—it's not going to taste good."

"Oh," I say, "right...I was just checking the temperature." But I think Billy catches on to the fact that I have no idea what suet is.

Then he explains so I don't feel so dumb. "Isn't it amazing how we can take a chunk of fat that used to surround the kidney of a cow and use it to feed birds?"

I try staying calm and hope I don't turn green. "It's unbelievable," I say (but I'm really thinking it's the most disgusting thing I've ever heard). I imagine the insides of a cow and visualize huge globs of fat packed around the kidney of a cow...which I'm pretty sure has something to do with the whole process of making pee.

Billy looks in the pan and seems satisfied. "There," he says. "One cup of suet completely melted. Now we need one cup of crunchy peanut butter." Billy measures it and dumps it in. "Okay," he says, "keep stirring." Then he adds two cups of oatmeal, two cups of cornmeal, and one cup of flour.

After it's mixed, Billy steadies the rectangular cake pan on the table, and I dump the massive glob in. We press it flat with bare hands (I use two, and Billy, one). "Eeewww," I say, cringing. "This feels disgusting. It's greasier than earwax."

Billy laughs hysterically. "I'm not sure about the earwax, but the peanut butter sure makes it smell good. The birds are going to love this!"

Once it's flat, Billy puts it in the fridge to cool and harden.

Next we make the hummingbird nectar. Billy starts by pouring four cups of water into a pan. Once it's boiling, he adds one cup of sugar. I stir until it dissolves. I scoop a little onto a teaspoon and blow on it. Since I'm absolutely sure it's only sugar and water (without an ounce of kidney fat), I bring it to my lips and sip. It tastes like liquid cotton candy.

"Want to hear something interesting?" Billy says. I look at him and wait because I know he's going to tell me either way. "A hummingbird's heart beats more than six hundred times a minute and a human's only beats about seventy-two." Billy's so smart.

I wonder if I'll ever be as smart as him.

13

Black Leather Boot

Billy pushes aside the branches as we walk into the woods. It feels cool and fresh after working in the hot kitchen.

"Hey, River, I almost forgot to tell you. My dad said he'll help us make the bluebird houses."

"That's great if you want an F. You heard Ms. Grackle—no parents."

"But it's for safety reasons, and he'd only cut the wood. There's no way he'd let us use the power saw."

"I guess you're right. That is great news."

As soon as we reach the field, Billy freezes. So I do the same thing. There are tiny birds at the feeder, and a bigger, bright red one right in the middle of the birdbath. We crouch, moving low along the ground like two Indian hunters until we reach the log, where we sit without a sound. Neither of us says a word. It's kind of a sacred moment. I can't believe there are birds. I never thought they'd come.

Billy whispers, "The red one's a northern cardinal. He's a male. Females aren't as colorful."

"Well, that's not fair."

Billy laughs and then leans close and whispers again. "The other birds at the feeder are black-capped chickadees. When they sing, they sound like they're saying their name. *Chick-a-dee-dee-dee, chick-a-dee-dee-dee.*"

Billy cracks me up.

It must have been his last *dee-dee* that made the birds fly away. But Billy says eventually they'll get used to people being around, and they'll stay longer. He takes a deep, satisfied breath and looks my way. "We'd better start watering," he says. "And I'm filling the bucket first."

As Billy positions himself at the edge of the bank, I start getting nervous. "You know, Billy, maybe we should listen to your father and get water from your house."

"He didn't say we had to get water from the house. He said he'd 'rather' we did."

"It's the same thing. And Gram doesn't like the idea of us using the bucket either."

"Don't worry, River. We'll be careful."

As I watch Billy throw the bucket over the edge, I hold my breath and have to force myself from grabbing onto his belt loop. But after a few minutes, I see he's doing fine, and he pulls a full bucket of water up over the edge. I let out my breath and remind myself that I didn't need to worry. I whisper the words from Matthew.

We water the seeds and fill the birdbath too. Then just as we're ready to go back and check the suet, Robert Killdeer comes by on his bike. He glares at Billy. "Hey," he says, "I was here 'bout an hour ago, and there was some ugly birds at your feeder."

Billy doesn't look at him.

Robert points to the bucket. "That yours?"

Billy nods.

Robert wanders over to it. "If you guys are getting water from the river, you're crazier than me. I wouldn't stand at this edge if you paid me." Then he steps on the bucket with his black leather boot and presses down on its side. He transforms the opening to an oval.

"Stop it!" I shout. "What do you think you're doing?"

Billy touches my arm. "It's okay, River."

Robert gives the bucket a kick. "If you was smart, you'd go down river where the bank ain't so steep."

I want to tell Robert there's no such word as 'ain't,' but I keep my mouth shut.

Robert spits, gets back on his bike, and rides away.

I search Billy's eyes for an answer.

"I don't want to talk about it," he says. Then he steps on the inside of the bucket and pulls on the squished side, trying to fix it. "Let's just go back to my house and see if the suet's hard."

$$\ast \ast \ast$$

Billy opens the fridge and pokes the suet with his finger. "Yep, it's hard just like we want." He puts the pan on the table. I hold it still while he cuts it into six perfectly square pieces (which he says are cakes). He places one inside the feeder. "Look at that. A perfect fit."

"Snug as a bug in a rug."

Billy laughs. "What did you say?"

"Snug as a bug in a rug...something Gram says."

We save the rest of the cakes in the fridge and then fill the hummingbird feeder. Billy steadies it over the sink while I pour the nectar. We make a pretty good team.

We carry the feeders to the birding place, and this time we see even more birds. Billy whispers, "We should've brought my camera."

"We'll remember next time."

While we're hanging the feeders, Mrs. Bunting comes by, carrying a cardboard box. "I was hoping you'd be here," she says. "Here's a patch of my Carolina phlox like I promised. And I brought you some daylilies too. Those ruby-throated hummingbirds will go crazy over them."

We thank Mrs. Bunting and tell her to come back soon.

* * *

Later when I get home, I find Gram sitting on the couch with a milk jug tied to her ankle, doing leg lifts (which somehow doesn't seem normal). And I'm pretty sure she reads my mind because she immediately starts explaining herself. "Just doing my exercises, Sugar Pie." Then she unties the jug from her ankle and stands up. "Whoooeee! Now that's good exercise!" As she walks to the kitchen with our milk, I notice she's not waddling as much as she used to. Maybe her physical therapist does know what he's doing.

"Glad you're home, Sugar Pie," she says in a singsong way, "'cause I've got a pot of stew that's brewing just for you!" Gram gets goofy like that sometimes, which never used to bother me when I was little. And it's too bad, really, because I've been thinking about inviting Billy over for lunch. But on account of Gram's peculiar ways and her physical therapist's harebrained ideas (plus the fact that we don't hold hands and pray before we eat), I decide I'd better not. I think I'd nearly die if I brought Billy home and Gram was galloping around the house or doing leg lifts with our milk jug. But maybe I will anyways. Billy's so nice—he probably wouldn't mind if she was.

14

··*·*·*·*·*·*·*·*·*·*·*·*·*·*·*

Hummingbird

uesday when school lets out, Billy runs over to me. "Hey, River, my dad cut the wood for our bluebird houses. Now all we have to do is nail the pieces together. Can you come over to work on them?"

"Sure. I'm not doing anything."

Billy's so excited he looks like he might burst. "These are going to be the coolest bluebird birdhouses ever!"

I figure I should tell Billy I haven't used a hammer before, except for when I was nine and tried helping Gram nail pieces of paneling to the walls in our living room. Gram was holding up the paneling and told me to pound the nail. But when I did, I accidently slammed the hammer clear through to the other side. Her face got redder than a hot pepper, and she said, "Sugar Pie, you'd better skedaddle. Get outside and take Paddles for a long walk. And you'd best stay out 'til the sun goes down." Later when I came home, there was a mirror hanging over the hole. I felt bad it was so close to the floor, but Gram just shook her head and said, "At least it's the right height for Paddles." Gram never could hold a grudge.

* * *

Billy and I take turns holding pieces of wood while the other one nails. First Billy holds and I hammer. The sides of the birdhouse go together first, and then the bottom. The front piece has a hole for a door, which is only the size of a quarter. It has to be small like that so squirrels can't get in. The last piece to go on is the roof, which is slanted like an obtuse triangle (and that is probably the only thing I remember from geometry).

I place my nail where I think it should go and lift my hammer, when all of a sudden, the wood moves. I look at Billy and say, "Can you please hold the pieces still?"

"I'm trying my best."

"Okay then, here I go." Instead of hitting the nail, I whack my thumb. "Ouch! That hurt!"

"Sorry, River. I'm having a hard time keeping the pieces still."

"It's not your fault," I say. And since Billy didn't ask to have only one hand that worked, I try making him feel better. "I just have really bad aim."

After we switch, I wonder how Billy's going to hold a nail and use the hammer with just one hand (and I sure don't want to hold the nail for him because I've already whacked my thumb enough). So I hold the pieces together for him and wait to see what happens.

"Watch this," he says, reaching up to a shelf where he finds a small wooden block with a hole in it. He takes the block, positions the hole where the nail should go, and makes sure it's balanced and steady. Then he lets go of the block and puts a nail inside the hole. He grabs his hammer and taps the nail—just enough so it's stuck in the wood. Then he lifts the block off. He grabs the hammer again and taps the nail, only harder this time. After a few hits, the nail's all the way in (even straighter than mine). Billy looks pleased. "My dad came up with that idea. Neat, isn't it?"

I nod. "Sure is."

After we finish our last bluebird house, we load them in the wagon and head back to the birding place. This time we remember Billy's camera.

* * *

Our seeds have sprouted, and they're growing like crazy. And the plants we were given are covered with blossoms (me and Billy know the secret to our green thumbs is the river water—it makes the plants very happy). We've got a flower for almost every color you can think of: pink coral bells, purple irises, and even a bunch of white angel coneflowers. We've already seen so many different kinds of birds and butterflies. With the nectar, suet cakes, birdseed, and all the flowers to choose from, this place must seem like heaven for them. You can bet that if I were a bird in Birdsong, I'd definitely be hanging out here.

But of all the birds I've seen, I like the hummingbirds best. They zip from one flower to another in a second, and disappear right before my eyes. And if I'm close enough, I can hear the sound of their wings beating and the cute chirping sounds they make.

We sit on the log and watch the birds for a while, which helps them get comfortable with us. Then we decide to start working on the rest of our project, so I begin taking notes while Billy takes pictures. My job is to write down any bird or butterfly behaviors I see, like what flowers they seem to like best, if they eat more seeds or suet, and if they get along with each other.

Billy positions his camera and tries getting close to three chickadees eating from the feeder, but they fly away. He moves back a little, then tries getting a picture while hiding behind the daylilies. All of a sudden, he yells, "River, come here!"

I drop my notes and run to him.

"Look!" he says and points. "There's a hummingbird stuck in that spider's web."

"Well, don't just stand there! Aren't you going to help it?"

He looks at me. "You should get to. Hummingbirds are your favorite."

"Wow! Thanks, Billy." I slowly move my hands toward the little bird, cup it gently, and pull it from the web. Then I position my hands between me and Billy so both of us will see. I open them. There in the palm of my hand sits a ruby-throated hummingbird. And it's beautiful. At first it doesn't move (Billy says that's because it's stunned), but then it turns its head to look at me, chirps once, and flies away.

"That was incredible, River. What did it feel like?"

"It was soft, like the silky edge on a baby blanket. And it hardly weighed a thing... It was like holding a marshmallow."

"Rats!" Billy says while holding up his camera. "I never took a picture!"

"That's okay," I tell him. "Maybe that was supposed to be something just for us to see. And I know I won't need a picture to remember."

We walk back to the log. Billy gets ready to take pictures again. There's a sparrow at the feeder, so he aims his camera and clicks the button. The camera spits the film out. He takes three more, and we watch them develop.

Billy looks discouraged. "My camera's not good enough. The pictures don't show enough detail. What we need is a camera with a powerful lens."

"What are we going to do? We've only got one week left."

Billy shrugs his shoulder. "I'm not sure yet." As we watch the birds, I hear Billy whisper, "God, please help us figure out something so we can get good pictures. My camera's nice, but it's not letting us get the kind of pictures I was hoping for... It would be really great to have pictures that show all the details of your amazing birds. I know you're good at figuring things out, so can you please help? Amen."

I turn to look at him. "Billy?"

"Yeah?"

"Do you think God really cares about our pictures? I mean, maybe he has bigger things to take care of...like making sure the earth keeps spinning or that the sun and moon hang in the right place. It seems like wanting good pictures for our project might not be that important to God."

"I get what you're saying, River, but God is actually so incredible and loves us so much that even though he has to take care of the big things, he wants to help us with our little things. My dad said we won't fully understand things like that until we get to heaven."

Just as Billy stops talking, we see two orange and black butterflies chasing each other near the bee balm.

"Those are monarchs," he says. "They're West Virginia's state butterfly."

"West Virginia has a state butterfly?"

"Yep, and now that you're living here, you need to know these things...so you're lucky you've got me to tell you about them." Billy smiles and says, "And do you want to know something else about them?"

"Sure, why not?" I say, because a person can't have too many butterfly facts floating around in their brain.

"Monarch butterflies migrate, just like birds. And the ones right here are the great grandchildren of the ones that lived in Mexico during the winter."

It takes me a few minutes to wrap my head around this whole butterfly thing because I'm not too smart when it comes to family ancestry and generational things (but maybe I would be if I knew where I came from).

As we keep watching the birds and butterflies, I'm getting more and more worried about our pictures. There's no chance we'll get an A without good pictures. I cross my fingers and make a wish that God was listening when Billy prayed.

All of a sudden, I hear loud *cawing* noises, and three big black birds land on the ground below the feeder. They caw and caw and chase the little chickadees away. "Stupid birds," I shout, waving my arms to shoo them, "go pick on someone your own size."

Even though I'm not trying to be funny, Billy laughs hysterically. "Actually," he says, taking control of himself, "crows are intelligent birds. People have even seen them take the rubber strips right off their windshield wipers."

"You're serious?"

"Of course I am," he says. "There's no way I could've made that up!"

I close my eyes and imagine Gram driving Tilly along an old country road when a humongous black crow comes out of nowhere and lands right in the middle of her windshield. Gram swerves all over, shouting at the top of her lungs, "Get out of here, you crazy old bird!" But the crow hangs on for dear life and pecks away at her wiper blades. Gram blasts Tilly's horn, and the crow flies away with her wiper blade clenched in his beak.

Billy jolts me back to reality, scaring me half to death. "I've got it!" he says. "My Uncle Jay's a photographer. Maybe he can help us."

"That's awesome. When do you think he can come over?"

"Well, there's one problem. He lives in Kentucky, and we don't see him much. But maybe he could come for a visit this weekend."

We race back to Billy's house and ask Pastor Henry.

15

Pinky Swear

After school on Friday, Billy and I hurry to the birding place. We want to make sure everything's perfect for the next morning when Billy's Uncle Jay will be here. We race each other to the end of the trail and then slowly creep out so we don't scare the birds. But this time we're the ones getting scared. We see birds all over the place—in the birdbath, at the feeder, and on the ground— but they're not moving. We walk closer to the bird feeder, where a lot of birds are lying. Then I look up and see shiny copper BBs lodged in the wood. They weren't there before. It takes a while for everything to register. It's like all the pieces of information are drifting around in my head, and then slowly, one by one, they line themselves up in order.

We walk over to the birdbath. There's a red cardinal in the water, still as can be. Billy lifts it out. It's stiff, just like the others.

They're dead.

"What's going on?" I say. Then for some reason, I imagine Robert Killdeer sitting on the log, looking down the barrel of a BB gun.

I turn toward Billy. A tear's sliding down his face. "I need to tell you something," he says, "but you have to promise you'll never tell a soul."

Even though I promise, Billy makes me pinky swear. We hook our left pinkies, and Billy whispers, "Pinky, pinky, grip real tight. A promise told will not lose hold, but break your word, you'll break our bond. It's pinky swear or death beware." Billy's face is pale, and he's shaking. He says, "I know who broke the church window."

"What?"

"One day last month, right before you moved here, I was outside at church sitting under the tree...reading a book, minding my own business. I'm sure Robert didn't even know I was there, but I was watching him because he was pacing back and forth, acting really strange. He didn't seem right. Then he picked up a rock and threw it through the window. It scared me half to death, so I jumped up, dropped my book, and ran. Robert came after me. He grabbed me by the neck and yanked me to his face. 'You better not tell, preacher boy,' he said, 'cuz if you do, I'll kill you!'"

I'm so scared, I can't move. "You never told?"

Billy shakes his head. "No way! I don't trust that kid. His dad's in jail. I heard he was charged with murder two days after Robert was born."

We sit there for a while, staring at nothing. Finally I say something. "What are we going to do with the birds?"

"We need to have a funeral. We can bury them behind the log. After that we never talk about this again, and we tell no one. Not ever."

We gently pick up the birds and carry them to the log. I count them. One cardinal, five chickadees, one goldfinch, four sparrows, two mourning doves, one woodpecker, and the most beautiful bluebird I've ever seen. I try to think of something good to help erase the bad stuff, but the only thing I can think of is how glad I am that hummingbirds fly faster than BBs.

We go back to Billy's house to get a shovel and his Bible.

* * *

I dig a hole for each bird while Billy flips through his Bible. I figure he's looking for something important, so I dig all fifteen holes myself. Billy finds a leaf and puts it in his Bible, like a bookmark.

As he picks up the bluebird, a feather falls from its wing and lands beside my foot. I pick it up and save it in my pocket. Later I'll put it in my diary with Paddles's feather. Billy sets the bluebird in its grave and then places the rest of the birds in their holes. I cover each of them. He saves the mourning doves for last and asks me to connect the last two holes. Billy says since mourning doves mate for life, they should be buried together. He lays them side by side, facing each other. I cover them with a blanket of dirt.

We stand beside each other, and Billy opens his Bible. "I'll read from Ecclesiastes, chapter three. 'For everything there is a season, a time for every activity under heaven. A time to be born and a time to die. A time to plant and a time to harvest. A time to kill and a time to heal. A time to tear down and a time to build up. A time to cry and a time to laugh. A time to grieve and a time to dance. A time to scatter stones and a time to gather stones. A time to embrace and a time to turn away. A time to search and a time to quit searching. A time to keep and a time to throw away. A time to tear and a time to mend. A time to be quiet and a time to speak. A time to love and a time to hate. A time for war and a time for peace.'"

Billy closes his Bible, then his eyes, and prays. "Dear Lord, thank you for this birding place and for your creation that comes to visit. I ask you to keep it safe and protect it from evil. And even though I'm so angry at Robert for what he's done, I know you want us to pray for our enemies. So even though I don't feel like it, I pray for Robert. Please help him find his way. Amen."

We gather leaves and sticks from the woods and lay them over the graves. No one will ever know.

16

* * * * * * * * * * * * * * * * * * *

Uncle Jay's Visit

The next morning I wake up before the sun and eat a quick bowl of Frosted Wheat Flakes. I don't waste time with a second because I need to get to Billy's. Gram's still sleeping (I know because I hear her snoring away down the hall). I set out a bowl, a spoon, and a coffee mug for her and then write a note reminding her where I'll be.

As soon as I reach Billy's house, warm smells of coffee and cinnamon rolls greet me at the screen door. It smells like a family. Pastor Henry, Billy, and his uncle are sitting at the table talking and laughing.

When Billy introduces me, his uncle looks at Pastor Henry and then back at me. "Your name is River?" he says. "I've heard that name only once before. How did your parents decide on River?"

There's no question that Pastor Henry and Uncle Jay are brothers—they look alike and even ask the same questions. Thank goodness Billy recues me before my stomach turns to tangled knots. "Here, Uncle Jay," he says and slides the plate of cinnamon rolls to him. "Have another one." Then Billy leans toward me and whispers, "You know, River, we need to come up with something you can tell people when they ask about your name."

I nod my head at Billy.

"Anyway, River," Billy's uncle says, "if you'd like, you can call me Uncle Jay too." He smiles and then slides the plate of cinnamon rolls toward me. I take the one loaded with the most frosting.

And then I can't believe it—Uncle Jay pours me a mug of coffee (I think I'm going to like having an uncle).

$$\star \star \star$$

Me and Billy and Uncle Jay each grab another cinnamon roll and head out for the birding place. Pastor Henry stays back to work on his Sunday message while the little Whippoorwills are still asleep and the house is quiet.

Uncle Jay brings his fancy camera that has at least six different lenses. Plus he has an amazing tripod (God sure didn't mess around when he answered Billy's prayer).

We let Uncle Jay lead the way through the woods, but me and Billy make sure we come out first. We want to make sure everything's safe. And it is. There are birds all over the place. And this morning they're moving.

While we sit on the log, Uncle Jay takes a few minutes to look around. "Your birding place is magnificent. Everywhere you look, there's color, texture, shading, form. It's a photographer's paradise." Then he glances at the sun coming over the horizon. "And with the soft morning light, I think you'll get some outstanding photos." He attaches his camera to the tripod and looks through the lens. He adjusts the height and then tells me and Billy what to do.

I have to catch my breath before I say, "You're letting us take pictures?"

Uncle Jay smiles, and when he does, I can't believe it. His is crooked too. He looks at me and says, "This is your project, isn't it?"

This might be the best day of my life.

I sit behind the tripod and get comfortable. First I focus the camera on the bird feeder and spot a black-capped chickadee eating seeds. I take its picture. Then I point the camera toward the suet feeder and focus on a woodpecker. I take its picture too. I even get pictures of two monarch butterflies sipping nectar from the Carolina phlox.

All of a sudden, we see a hummingbird near the bee balm. Uncle Jay quickly removes the lens and exchanges it with one that's super long. "Here, River. Try this."

I place my eye against the camera and see a beautiful ruby-throated hummingbird hovering in midair. It looks like a shimmering scoop of key-lime sherbet with a raspberry tucked under its chin.

Uncle Jay says to take as many pictures as we want. I think I've taken ten.

When it's Billy's turn, he focuses on the birdbath. Then he waits. And waits some more. He's hoping to see a thirsty bird or one that needs a bath (Billy's more patient than I could ever be). Pretty soon a cardinal lands on the edge and takes a drink. Billy clicks the camera. I bet it'll be an awesome picture. Then we see two mourning doves feeding on the ground, and Billy takes their picture too.

All of a sudden, Billy whispers, "Wow, look!" He turns the camera toward two bluebirds. Their feathers are beautiful. As we watch, the male raises and quivers one of his wings and feeds his mate a morsel of food (maybe that is my idea of romance, after all). Billy clicks the camera sixteen times.

Next we see a goldfinch land on the tallest sunflower, making it sway back and forth. The finch's yellow feathers blend in with the sunflower so at first it's hard to see. It pecks at the seeds, looks around, and chirps *po-ta-to-chip*.

I just about die laughing. "Did you hear that? It sounded like it said potato chip!"

Billy grins. "Amazing, isn't it? That's actually its contact call. Goldfinches use it to keep in touch with their friends."

Uncle Jay laughs and shakes his head. "Unbelievable!"

But what I can't believe is that now I have an uncle.

17

$\star \ast_\star \ast_\star \star_\star \ast \star_\star \ast_\star \star \ast_\star \ast_\star \star \ast_\star \ast_\star \star \ast_\star \ast_\star \star$

Saving Gram

$\mathcal{A}$fter school on Thursday, me and Billy race to his mailbox. He beats me, opens the lid, and shouts, "I knew it! Uncle Jay mailed them right away, just like he promised!"

I jump up and down like a little kid. "And it's perfect timing! We've got four days 'til our project's due, so we've got just enough time."

We run toward Billy's house, when all of a sudden, he stops. "Can we go to your house and look at them? If we stay here, my brothers and sisters will climb all over them."

"Sure," I say, "we can go to my house if you want." But inside I whisper, "God, please make sure Gram isn't doing something strange."

In ten minutes we're at my house, spreading our pictures across the kitchen table. Gram's in the living room practicing her banjo (which is better than exercising with our milk jug), but I'm still relieved when she stops twanging "Oh! Susanna" and waddles over to see our pictures.

Gram's face beams while she looks at the pictures. She tells us how she's had a love for birds since the day Gramp proposed to her (even though I've heard this story a thousand times, I still like listening). "It's gotta be a good forty-eight years since River's grand-daddy proposed to me. Course River wasn't even around back then. Well, he'd gone out and bought an African gray parrot without

81

saying a word about it to me, and he taught that bird to say, 'Will you marry me?'" Gram chuckles and grabs hold of her belly. "That man was more fun than a fox in a henhouse. I have no idea how a girl could've said no!"

I think that's probably why she found room in her big old heart for Paddles, even though that crazy duck couldn't talk or do a trick to save its life. But I guess when it comes right down to it, a bird's a bird.

Billy can't take his eyes off the pictures. "These are incredible! They look like they should be in *National Geographic*."

"By George, you're right," Gram says.

"You know," Billy says, "Uncle Jay used to take pictures for that magazine. He'd travel all over the world taking pictures, and the magazine would publish them. But that was quite a while ago—around the time I was born. My parents still have a stack of them in the attic. Sometimes I go up there and look at them, imagining I was with him on those trips."

"Why'd he stop?" Gram asks.

Billy gets a serious look on his face. "On his last trip, something terrible happened. So after that he stopped taking pictures for a long time."

"Well, what happened?" Gram says. "The suspense is darn near killing me."

"He was on a photo assignment, and that time he decided to bring his wife and baby along."

"Wait a minute," I say. "I didn't know Uncle Jay has a wife and kid."

"Well, he used to."

"Go on," Gram says.

"Well, he was at the Eisenhower National Historic Site in Pennsylvania when—"

Gram interrupts Billy and looks at me. "Your mom and daddy

used to live around them parts." Then she apologizes to Billy and tells him to go on.

"Uncle Jay was taking pictures when his wife had to go to the bathroom. She asked him to watch the baby, but Uncle Jay never heard her. When she came back, their baby was gone."

Gram closes her eyes. "That's the saddest thing I've ever heard." She gets real quiet and lets out a sigh. "Did they ever find that baby?"

Billy shakes his head. "The police searched for years but didn't have any luck. I was so young at the time, and no one ever talks about it, so I don't know very much about it. Anyway, after that Uncle Jay's wife left him. But even after all those years, Uncle Jay still carries a picture of them in his wallet."

Gram gets a puzzled look on her face and says to Billy, "I'd like to see that picture sometime." Then she shakes her head a few times and looks out the kitchen window toward our mailbox. "Well, I'm gonna see if the postmaster brought me anything exciting too. You never know what the day's gonna bring." She heads out, letting the screen door slam behind her.

I sort through the hummingbird pictures, looking for my favorite. "You know, Billy," I say, "today could be my lucky day. There just might be a letter from my parents waiting in the mailbox." I look out the window and see Gram hopping down the driveway on one foot—she might as well be on a pogo stick. I try distracting Billy so he doesn't look out the window.

We sort a few more pictures, when I look out the window again. This time Gram isn't hopping. She's lying at the edge of the road, right beside our mailbox. At first I wait to see if she's doing some crazy exercise, but when she doesn't move, I yell for her and run outside. Billy hurries behind me.

I lift Gram's head, but her eyes stay closed. Billy runs back toward the house, yelling over his shoulder, "I'll call an ambulance!"

"Our phone's been shut off!" I yell back. "Just get Tilly's keys." Billy freezes, so I yell again, "Get the keys!"

I check Gram's pulse, remembering what Billy said about a hummingbird's heart beating six hundred times a minute and a human's beating seventy-two times. I haven't counted one on Gram.

I grab the keys from Billy and slip behind Tilly's steering wheel, trying to remember everything I've watched Gram do. I put the key in, turn it, and push on the gas. Tilly starts on the first try. I shift into reverse, push on the gas, and the truck jerks backward toward the mailbox. I shift into park, get out, and open Tilly's tailgate. I yell for Billy to help. Somehow we manage to get Gram in. I shove Billy in the back too and tell him to stay with her. I slam Tilly's tailgate shut and climb back in the driver's seat.

Billy's voice is trembling. "What are you going to do?"

"I'm driving to your house. We need a grown-up to get Gram to the hospital."

"That won't work," he says. "My dad's at church, and my mom can't leave the kids."

I tell myself I can do this, shift into drive, point Tilly in the direction of the church, and press on the gas. As I look in the rear-view mirror, I meet Billy's eyes. I can tell he's crying. I yell through the glass, "Have you ever done CPR?"

"I've only seen it on TV."

"That's all right," I tell him. "Do the same thing. Push down in the middle of Gram's chest a bunch of times. Then tip her head back and plug her nose so you can blow air into her lungs. You have to blow twice." I look in the mirror again and see him trying, but it doesn't look like it's going well.

"I'm sorry!" Billy yells. "I don't think I'm doing good enough."

I forgot about his arm. I pull Tilly over to the side of the road and tell Billy to switch with me.

His voice is panicky. "I've never driven before."

"We don't have time to worry about that. You just have to do it." I jump in the back of Tilly, next to Gram, and push on her chest hard and fast. "Come on, Gram. You can't leave me." I tip her head back, plug her nose, and then blow two big breaths into her lungs. Breaths of life. No death, Gram, only life. I do it over and over and over.

When we reach the church, Billy gets out and runs for help while I keep trying to save Gram. Before I know it, Pastor Henry's in the driver's seat, squealing Tilly's wheels, and racing to the hospital. When we get there, he backs Tilly up to the emergency department, and a bunch of doctors and nurses rush out to help. They lift Gram out of Tilly, place her on a stretcher, and wheel her away before I can tell her goodbye.

I'm still on my knees in the back of Tilly, crying harder than I ever knew I could.

* * *

Pastor Henry, Billy, and I sit in the waiting room. There must not be any other emergencies in Birdsong today because we're the only ones waiting. And that's a good thing because there's only three chairs.

Pastor Henry puts his hand on my shoulder. "Would you like me to pray for your grandmother?"

I nod. I figure if God helped us get an awesome camera when Billy prayed, then God will definitely help Gram if Pastor Henry prays.

The three of us hold hands. Since Billy's at my left, I take hold of the hand on his dangling arm (which I've never touched before). It's soft, warm, and squishy—kind of like pizza dough.

Pastor Henry bows his head. "Dear heavenly Father, we need your help. We ask that you be with River's grandmother and that you'd give the doctors wisdom as they make medical decisions. And if it be your will, we ask that you'd keep her with us for many years to come. But if you choose to take her, we ask for the strength to go on. We pray this in your name. Amen."

I have to be honest. Even though I'm grateful Pastor Henry prayed, I actually think it would've made more sense to just ask God to make her better. Because, really, that's what I need.

Pastor Henry takes my hand. "River," he says softly, "God doesn't always answer our prayers like we want. We can pray for things to turn out a certain way, but the decision is ultimately up to him…and we won't always understand that. But because God is God, we need to trust that his ways are good."

I nod, trying to understand, but there's no space left in my brain for that because there are two very big thoughts taking up all the space: the first is wondering if Gram will get better, and the second is knowing my parents need to find me fast. If Gram doesn't make it, I'll have no one.

Pastor Henry leans back in his chair, staring out the window. Then all of a sudden, he sits up straighter than a two-by-four and starts asking a million questions (I think he finally realized Billy drove Gram's truck). "How much traffic was there? Did you stop at the main intersection and look both ways? Did you even consider how dangerous that was? What would you have done if you got in an accident?"

Billy looks scared to death. He's probably wondering what Pastor Henry's going to do. And all I can do is sit here wondering if Billy's ever been grounded before.

* * *

Gram's doctor pushes the waiting room door open and walks straight at me. My whole body's tight, and everything inside me is shaking. I don't want to hear what he says, but he bends down right in front of me so I don't have a choice. "She's a lucky lady to have a granddaughter like you," he says. "If you hadn't done CPR and gotten here as fast as you did, she wouldn't have had a chance." My body can't make up its mind—it shakes, it cries, it laughs, and it cries some more. It's never had to make so many decisions.

The doctor says Gram needs to stay overnight so he can monitor her and make changes to her heart medicine. As he starts to leave, he turns around. "You know," he says, "your grandmother started to explain what happened. She said she was hopping down the driveway to get her mail, but then she closed her eyes and fell asleep. She never finished explaining. Anyway, I thought the whole hopping thing sounded strange, so I'm wondering if you have any idea why she would've been hopping when most folks her age walk."

I tell him about her nincompoop therapist.

18

* ★ * ★ * ★ * ★ * ★ * ★ * ★ * ★ * ★ * ★ * ★ * ★ *

A Plan of Our Own

One good thing about Gram being in the hospital is that I get to spend the night at the Whippoorwills'.

When Billy and I read the little Whippoorwills a story before bed, they beg us to read a Bible story about a giant fish that swallowed a guy named Jonah. It's an interesting story (and Billy swears it's true). The story begins with God asking Jonah to do something, but since Jonah doesn't want to do it, he tries running away from God (which is a stupid thing to do if you ask me). Jonah thinks he outsmarts God and takes the first boat out of town (that's because they didn't have cars back then). But God doesn't let Jonah get away, and he makes a storm happen. When the waves become wild, Jonah gets tossed overboard and swallowed by a giant fish (Jonah actually stays in its stomach for three days). Well, Jonah finally gets smart. He asks God for a second chance, and lucky for him, he gets one. God tells the fish to spit Jonah out on shore, which it did (even the fish knew enough to obey God). Sometimes people have to learn the hard way.

After we finish the story, I help tuck the little Whippoorwills into bed. Each one of them says a prayer for Gram. Even little Forrest.

★ ★ ★

In the morning Mrs. Whippoorwill makes everyone breakfast. She has a huge pot of oatmeal simmering on the stove, she's poured a whole jug of orange juice into a counter full of glasses, and she's used an entire loaf of bread to make the tallest stack of toast I've ever seen.

Pastor Henry takes a piece of toast off the top and wipes the last bit of oatmeal from his bowl. He says to me, "I'll bring your grandmother home from the hospital at eleven this morning. That will give her time to rest before you get home from school."

I don't think Pastor Henry knows Gram that much because Gram's not real good at resting. Even if the doctor gives her strict orders to stay in bed, she's bound to start up with all her hopping, galloping, milk-jug-leg-lifting, ballet moves (and heaven only knows what else).

Billy and I ask Pastor Henry if we can go with him, since we want to bring Gram home too, but he shakes his head and insists we go to school.

When asking doesn't work, we beg.

He shakes his head and says, "Not a chance."

* * *

I try sitting through math class, but I can't concentrate. I couldn't care less about long division. All I want is to get Gram and bring her home.

Later during English, Ms. Grackle instructs us to sit with our partners. "By the end of this class," she says, "the goal is to have your project essay completely outlined and approved by me." But Billy and I come up with our own plan (which is definitely not the same as Ms. Grackle's). We suddenly (and suspiciously) come down with terrible stomachaches, so Ms. Grackle sends us straight to the nurse. Billy and me walk down the hall, holding our stomachs and making the best groaning noises we can. We reach the nurse's office, gripping our stomachs and bending over in pain.

Billy talks first. "Miss Nightingale, River and I don't feel good. Our stomachs feel awful."

I give Miss Nightingale more information. "I think it has something to do with breakfast."

"She's probably right," Billy says. "We drank sour orange juice, ate toast made with moldy bread, and our oatmeal was horribly lumpy." I nod my head and agree.

Miss Nightingale scrunches her nose like she'd just stepped on a dead mouse. "Well," she says, "there's no doubt about it—the both of you need to go home immediately." She picks up the phone while asking Billy for his number.

"That's okay, Miss Nightingale," he says. "There's no need to call my parents. I don't want to be a bother to them. My mom's home with all the little ones, and my dad's busy preparing Sunday's message. I can walk home."

When Miss Nightingale asks for my number, I explain, "Gram couldn't pay the phone bill, so ours is shut off" (this is true, so just like Gram, I didn't lie...except about my stomachache...and I also agreed it was caused by sour orange juice, moldy toast, and lumpy oatmeal). I wonder if God forgives people if they have a good reason to lie.

Billy assures Miss Nightingale, "You don't need to worry about River. I'll walk with her and see that she gets home safely."

She pats Billy on his head. "You're a real gentleman." Then she hands us a pass to leave school and says she hopes we feel better.

As soon as we walk out the front doors, our stomachaches disappear, and we feel one hundred percent better. We race down the steps. I glance back over my shoulder, hoping we don't get snared by the falcon.

* * *

We're halfway home when I get the brainstorm about making Gram a welcome-home lunch. And I know exactly what she needs—chicken noodle soup, bologna sandwiches, and a tall glass of groundhog punch.

Billy scratches his head. "Groundhog punch?"

"You've never heard of it?" For once I get to teach Billy something. "It's a magic punch that Punxsutawney Phil drinks each year. That's why he lives a long time. So I bet if Gram drinks some, she'll live a long time too."

Billy nods. "That's an interesting thought."

I take a few more steps. "But there's one problem."

"What's that?"

I hesitate to tell, since I'm not sure Billy believes in the whole magic punch theory, but I go ahead anyway. "We can't make it because the recipe is top secret."

"Well," Billy says, "why don't we come up with our own magical punch recipe? We could use your Gram's favorite drinks as the ingredients and then mix them together. If groundhog punch works for Punxsutawney Phil, then maybe our recipe will work for Gram."

As I shoot Billy a smile, he takes my lead. We race down the road and around the corner to Quick-Shop to buy Gram's favorite drinks (I can't help thinking how smart we were to leave school before lunch, otherwise we wouldn't have any lunch money).

We grab a cart and race through the aisles. I toss in lemon-lime soda, a carton of cranberry juice, orange juice, and pineapple juice, and then a family-size can of chicken noodle soup. We don't buy Berry Burst Drink Mix because Gram's always stocked up on that.

After paying we have ten cents left, so I slide the dime to the cashier and grab two red-hot fireballs.

* * *

By the time we get to my house, it's ten forty, and our fireballs are the size of a pea. Billy hurries to set the table, and then I ask him to make seven bologna sandwiches (Gram will definitely have a big appetite).

I heat the soup, let it simmer, and then get ready to make our magical punch. I slide our stool to the cupboard and climb up. I reach for Gram's special glass pitcher, hoping the whole time I don't drop it because it means so much to her. She won it by mailing seven hundred Berry Burst Drink Mix labels to the company and being the one lucky person to have their name drawn (I'll bet she was the only entrant because I don't think anyone else would be crazy enough to save seven hundred Berry Burst labels). But everyone in Punxsutawney knew Gram wanted that glass pitcher, so we'd always find Berry Burst labels tucked under our door. Gram ended up saving all seven hundred labels in just two weeks. She was happier than a pig in mud when it arrived in the mail. When we packed to move, I saw her wrap eleven towels around it (so even if the movers used it to play football, there was no chance of it breaking). Gram only uses it on special occasions, but I think her coming home with a beating heart is definitely special.

I measure one cup of orange juice, cranberry juice, pineapple juice, and Gram's favorite Berry Burst drink and pour it into her pitcher. Then I add the entire can of lemon-lime soda. And finally I drop in twelve ice cubes and stir it around and around until it creates a magical whirlpool. I take a sip from the spoon and smile— the magic already makes my tongue tingle. I carry the pitcher to the table and carefully set it down, feeling happy that something this simple might actually help Gram live a whole lot longer.

As soon as Billy finishes the bologna sandwiches, we hear the sound of tires in the driveway. Two seconds later Gram and Pastor Henry walk through the door.

Me and Billy shout, "Surprise! Welcome home!"

Gram nearly jumps out of her skin, "Oh, my stars! You scared the kajeebers outta me!" She laughs a big belly laugh and then waddles over and gives us each a bear hug. "You kids saved my life, and I can't thank you enough. The doctor adjusted my heart medicine, and now my ticker's good as new. And boy, do I feel terrific!" As soon as she spots the food, she releases her hug and skips to the table with the grace of a hungry hippopotamus. She sits down with a thump.

Pastor Henry sure looks surprised...probably not so much at Gram's skipping as at seeing me and Billy standing in the middle of the kitchen. And he definitely doesn't seem happy about it.

He glares at Billy. "What in the world are you doing here?" (I'm thinking if Pastor Henry didn't ground Billy yesterday for driving Tilly, this might be a perfect opportunity). "Aren't you supposed to be in school, young man?"

Billy shrugs his shoulder. Now, since I believe friends should always rescue each other, I put my hands together like an angel and look at Pastor Henry. "You're invited too! Everyone likes chicken noodle soup and bologna sandwiches, so you're going to stay and eat, right?"

His eyes stay glued on Billy. "No," he says, "I'm afraid not. I have responsibilities at the church." I consider telling Pastor Henry about our magical punch, but this doesn't seem like good timing.

Pastor Henry is still glaring. "Billy," he says, "the minute you're done eating, you're to come directly to the church. You'll spend the afternoon polishing every pew. And if you take too long getting there, you'll have the opportunity to polish them twice."

After Pastor Henry leaves, I ask Billy what a pew is. He says they're the benches we've been sitting on (I'm relieved because with the sound of a word like "pew," I had visions of Billy polishing every toilet in the church. Lucky for Billy they're benches).

Gram gobbles her bologna sandwiches, slurps up her soup, and then guzzles three big glasses of our magical punch. "Whoooeeee!" she shouts. "That's the best drink I've ever had!"

I figure those three glasses of punch just added a whole lot of years to her life. Plus she'll probably drink what's left in the pitcher before she goes to bed. So, with all that punch and me praying for her every night, I think Gram will be around for a real long time.

Billy eats his bologna sandwich in fast-forward motion, says see you later, and runs out the door (I'm sure he doesn't want to polish twice).

Gram actually decides to lie down for an afternoon snooze, so I decide to make the labels for our display. Monday will be here before we know it.

19

* *

Good Ears

Saturday morning as I'm finishing my bowl of Frosted Wheat Flakes, I see Billy walking up our driveway (at least today he slept in later than the birds). He's carrying Pastor Henry's typewriter, which looks like it weighs as much as he does, and so I hurry and open the door for him. "Morning, Billy. Want me to grab that?"

"No, that's okay. I've got it." He sets the typewriter on the table and sits beside me.

I hold our project labels out for Billy to see. "Look what I made yesterday while you were busy shining pews."

"Wow, River! They look great! Thanks for doing them." He puts a piece of paper in the typewriter. "Well, should we do our essay first?"

"I suppose...we might as well get the torture over with."

"Oh, come on, River. Essays aren't that bad," he says. "I'm thinking that since you've got two good hands, you should do the typing. You'll type twice as fast."

"Fine with me," I say, "and since you have twice the brains, you can tell me what to type."

Billy laughs. "Fair is fair."

I take in a deep breath. "Okay, if our essay needs to be two hundred and fifty words and I can type about five words a minute, how long is this going to take?"

Billy shifts into teacher mode. "Well, think of this as a math problem. If you type five words a minute, simply divide two hundred and fifty by five to see how many minutes it will take." He waits a minute and then looks at me like I should know. "Well?"

"Well, what?" I say. "You're the one with twice the brains."

"But you're the one who wants to know."

I scribble a few numbers on scrap paper. "Fifty minutes?"

"Perfect, but that accounts only for your typing. We need to add some time for me to read our notes, think about them, and put everything together."

"With a brain like yours, we only need to add three minutes."

"Give me a break, River—I'm not that smart!"

✳ ✳ ✳

Ninety minutes later I type the last word of our essay. I press the caps lock key and type *THE END* at the bottom of the page. But when Billy sees it, his eyes bug out. "I don't think you need to type that! Ms. Grackle's been a teacher for a real long time, and I'm sure she knows when an essay ends."

"But it's like an exclamation mark shouting, 'We're done!' Besides, it makes me feel good...like I finally accomplished something important."

"Well, if it makes you that happy, we should keep it."

Miss Nightingale is right. Billy is a gentleman.

✳ ✳ ✳

As we sort our photos, Gram comes back from her morning walk along the river. She bursts through the screen door, leans her hiking stick in the corner of the kitchen, and hollers, "God Almighty, that's one beautiful morning out there!"

My face gets instantly hot, and I'm totally embarrassed. I'm pretty sure it's sinful to say "God Almighty" like that, but Billy didn't flinch. Maybe he's too caught up in our project to notice, or maybe he's just being polite. But when I look again, I can see he's holding back a crooked, little half grin.

Gram wipes the sweat off her brow, waddles over to me, and rubs my head. "How's my sugar pie this morning?" Then she looks at Billy. "And how's Billy? Sorry 'bout your dad having you polish all those pews yesterday. Don't get me wrong. I respect your daddy one hundred percent, but if it was me, I wouldn't have made you do it. That's because I loved having you here to welcome me home." Then she waddles over to Billy and rubs his head. "Now, don't you tell Pastor Henry on me," she says and chuckles, "or he might not let me come back to church."

Billy laughs at Gram. "You don't need to worry about that. He's never closed the doors on anyone. He's just strict sometimes, especially when it comes to school or telling the truth. Besides, I deserved it. I shouldn't have lied and skipped school, even if it was for a good reason. Those pews needed a good shine, anyways. Wait until you see them."

Gram looks at me. "What do you say, Sugar Pie?"

"About what?"

"You want to go to church again tomorrow and see those shiny pews?"

I don't hesitate for a second to tell her yes. But my excitement hits the floor when she opens the fridge and pulls out the milk jug. I hold my breath. "God," I whisper inside, "please don't let her do leg lifts with that." And at that very moment, I learn God has extremely good ears because Gram sets the milk jug on the table instead of tying it to her ankle. Then she opens the cupboard and grabs three tall glasses along with her tin of chocolate-chip cookies.

* * * * * * * * * * * * * * * * * *

20

A Father Who Loves Me

On Sunday morning Pastor Henry pulls their big white van into our driveway, just like he did last week. And as soon as Gram and I hop inside, the little Whippoorwills flock around us. I love the feel of them climbing all over me (and I'm pretty sure Gram does too). First Gram gives each of the girls a ride on her knee as she sings out, "This is the way the ladies ride, the ladies ride, the ladies ride. This is the way the ladies ride all the way to church!" It makes me remember when I was small enough to sit on her knee.

Then she gives each of the boys a ride, but she changes the words to, "This is the way the gentlemen ride, the gentlemen ride, the gentlemen ride. This is the way the gentlemen ride all the way to church!"

* * *

We walk into church, and every one of us is greeted with a hug. Gram parks herself beside the donut table and eats enough to last her the week. I take only one. After all, Jesus is guarding them (I don't think Gram noticed).

Billy and I stay with Gram near the donut table, and everyone who comes over has something nice to say about the birding place. Mrs. Martin, our lunch lady, says she can't believe how big her bee balm has grown and wants to know what our secret is. Billy and

I don't say a word about the river water, so we all agree it must be the music of the birds (Mrs. Martin says a flower only grows when a bird sings).

All of a sudden, Mrs. Martin moves in super close and positions her face at my ear. She whispers, "I thought you should know that our milk suppliers are all out of chocolate." Her words feel like a swarm of buzzing mosquitos near my ear, but I keep myself from swatting at her. Then she buzzes again, "But no need to worry because I hid every carton we had left, and I'm going to make sure you get chocolate milk every single day this week." My mosquito swatting thoughts disappear.

Mrs. Bunting comes over next. She tells us how much she enjoys the birding place and that she can't believe how well her daylilies and blue phlox are doing. "One day last week," she says, "I was sitting on the log saying my prayers when I counted nine hummingbirds! Can you imagine! I've never seen so many hummingbirds all at once!" Then she wraps her arms around Billy and me and gives us a Sunday squeeze. "There's something special about that birding place."

I drink the last sip of Gram's coffee before we head to the big part of the church (which today I learn is called a "sanctuary"). And I like that word because if you say it real slow (like sank-chu-ary), it has a very holy sound about it.

We sit on the same bench as last Sunday. I decide that even though they're technically called pews, I'm still going to call them benches. I don't think a word like pew is nice enough for a place like this. After all, Pastor Henry says this is God's house.

Pastor Henry stands up front again. This morning he has a mile-wide smile spread across his face (he must've forgotten all about me and Billy skipping school, or maybe he's just happy to see the pews so shiny). He asks us to open our hymnals and join with him in singing "The Solid Rock." I'm glad the piano lady doesn't have a microphone in front of her because her voice is plenty loud without one (plus she clearly doesn't have the kind of voice you'd want to broadcast).

I stand beside Billy, and we share a hymnal. He's so lucky he can read music. I follow along and listen, hoping maybe I can learn too.

When the song ends, Pastor Henry asks us to sing it once more. He wants us to pay attention to the words. This time I try and sing along too.

> My hope is built on nothing less
> Than Jesus' blood and righteousness.
> I dare not trust the sweetest frame,
> But wholly lean on Jesus' name.
>
> On Christ, the solid Rock, I stand,
> All other ground is sinking sand;
> All other ground is sinking sand.
>
> When darkness seems to hide His face,
> I rest on His unchanging grace.
> In ev'ry high and stormy gale,
> My anchor holds within the veil.
>
> His oath, His covenant, His blood,
> Support me in the whelming flood.
> When all around my soul gives way,
> He then is all my Hope and Stay.
>
> When He shall come with trumpet sound,
> Oh, may I then in Him be found!
> Dressed in His righteousness alone,
> Faultless to stand before the throne!

On Christ, the solid Rock, I stand,
All other ground is sinking sand;
All other ground is sinking sand.

Even though I don't understand every single word, I really like this song (and I'll bet Gram will be singing it all week while she's galloping, skipping, and hopping around our house).

Pastor Henry opens his Bible. "This morning we'll read from the book of James. This is what he writes: 'Come now, you who say, "Today or tomorrow we will go into such and such a town and spend a year there and trade and make a profit"—yet you do not know what tomorrow will bring. What is your life? For you are a mist that appears for a little time and then vanishes. Instead you ought to say, "If the Lord wills, we will live and do this or that."'"

Pastor Henry clears his throat, then closes his Bible. "James is saying that our lives are short. They're here and gone like a mist, a vapor, or a puff of smoke" (I wish Pastor Henry didn't mention that part about the puff of smoke because if Gram's paying any attention, she might be tempted to start up again). Gram must have read my mind because she pats me on my knee and whispers, "Now, don't go worrying yourself, Sugar Pie."

Pastor Henry looks back and forth across the sanctuary. "We can plan our lives, and there's nothing wrong with that, but we need to include God. When we do, he'll set the course. But sometimes he changes the course in a direction we'd never expect." Pastor Henry holds his Bible close to his chest, like it's his favorite book in the whole world. "We can only see from one moment to the next, but God knows our life from before its beginning all the way through to its end...and since we never know when that will be, we need to be ready."

Someone from the back of the church shouts, "Amen!" I turn around and see Mrs. Martin with her arms raised to the ceiling, but I keep myself from snickering because I'm counting on that chocolate milk.

Pastor Henry steps down from the stage and stands right in front of everyone who's in the first row (I'm glad I'm sitting three rows back). All of a sudden, he gets a serious look on his face. "What would happen if you were in a car wreck on the way home from church today and you didn't survive? Do you know where you'd spend eternity? Would it be heaven? Or would it be hell? God lets us make that choice. He made it so easy for us to spend eternity with him in heaven...and he doesn't want anyone to miss out."

I hear Mrs. Martin shout amen again, but this time she's annoying me because I want to hear what Pastor Henry has to say, even more than I want chocolate milk. With Gram almost dying, it got me thinking about life and death and all that stuff.

Pastor Henry explains, "God gave his son, Jesus, to die on the cross for us. He did that in exchange for our sins. He says there's not one person on earth who hasn't sinned." Now I'm getting warmer by the minute, and I'll bet my face is redder than a hot tamale because all I can think of is how I lied about my stomachache, the sour orange juice, moldy toast, and lumpy oatmeal. But I keep listening because I really want to hear.

Pastor Henry's voice turns soft and gentle. "But there's good news. When we ask God to forgive us, he does. We're completely clean—a whole new creation. It's that simple. And," he says, "it gets even better. God is your heavenly father and loves you more than you could imagine. He loves you like no one ever has or ever will. And he will never leave you."

All I've ever wanted is to be part of a real family and to have a father who loves me. So since my real parents haven't found me yet and my adoptive parents haven't come back, maybe having a heavenly father will do just fine until then. I'm sure it's okay to have a heavenly father and an earthly one both at the same time.

The whole church is silent (even Mrs. Martin) when the piano lady tiptoes over to the piano. She begins playing softly. Her hands move back and forth across the keys in slow motion, which actually looks a bit dramatic.

Pastor Henry asks us to sing one of his favorite hymns, "Come to the Savior, Make No Delay." This time I begin singing on the first word and don't worry if I know the song or not.

> Come to the Savior, make no delay;
> Here in His Word He has shown us the way;
> Here in our midst He's standing today,
> Tenderly saying, "Come!"
>
> Joyful, joyful will the meeting be,
> When from sin our hearts are pure and free;
> And we shall gather, Savior, with Thee,
> In our eternal home.

Pastor Henry stops singing before the song's even over. "If there's anyone who would like to have a heavenly father, I invite you to come up front with me." Then he adds, "There's no need to worry what anyone else will think. Now we'll sing the last two verses, and then the service will end."

> "Suffer the children!" oh, hear His voice!
> Let ev'ry heart leap forth and rejoice;
> And let us freely make Him our choice;
> Do not delay, but come.
>
> Think once again, He's with us today;
> Heed now His blest command, and obey;
> Hear now His accents tenderly say,
> "Will you, My children, come?"

All of a sudden, my body stands up, and I feel myself walk to the front of the church. It's like I'm being pulled by a giant magnet.

Then before I know it, I realize Gram's standing on one side of me and Billy's on the other. And if I didn't know better, I'd swear Pastor Henry has tears in his eyes.

Pastor Henry smiles at me and Gram. "I'm very glad you came forward," he says, "and I can only imagine how all of heaven is rejoicing." Then he looks at Billy. "Did you come to support River?"

Billy shakes his head. "I want to make sure I'm ready too."

Pastor Henry puts his arm around Billy's shoulder. "You made a decision to follow God when you were five, Billy. You don't need to do it again."

"I know, Dad, but I was little then. I'm older now. And even though God doesn't need me to do it again, I want to."

Pastor Henry squeezes Billy's shoulder. "Well, that's certainly fine."

Pastor Henry leads us in a prayer. He says we can repeat it out loud if we want. All three of us do.

After we finish praying, I have the most amazing thought—I finally have a father who loves me.

21

★ * ★ * ★ * ★ * ★ * ★ * ★ * ★ * ★ * ★ * ★ * ★ * ★

Presentation Day

Ms. Grackle greets everyone Monday morning with a huge smile. And since it's Project Presentation Day, she's dressed as if she were having dinner with the president of the United States. She's squeezed up tight in a sparkly purple dress and is wearing purple sparkly shoes, lipstick, and nail polish to match. Plus, she's wearing earrings that dangle all the way to her shoulders (I definitely think she went overboard).

She taps a ruler on her desk. "Since each one of you has worked incredibly hard and very diligently on your projects, I've invited Mr. Sparrow's class to join us for your presentations. I'm quite pleased, to say the least. I've never had a class who's taken their projects as seriously as you, so I wanted to do something extra special for you." The classroom grows dead silent. I think everyone was expecting something more.

Within seconds Mr. Sparrow's class walks through the door. The rotten thing is, there are so many students that we have to double up on our seats, which seems more like a punishment.

As Ms. Grackle introduces our first presenters, Mr. Sparrow raises his hand and asks if she could wait a minute. He said he has one more student coming. Then three seconds later, Robert Killdeer walks through the door. Billy and I look at each other (and I wonder if his heart is beating as fast as a hummingbird's too).

Once Robert finds half a chair to sit on, Ms. Grackle click-clacks her way to the door and closes it. Then she click-clacks back to the front of the room, all the while shimmering like a jar of grape jelly. She introduces Sam and Joel, who did their project on stamp collecting. They pass around stamps from all over the world. They do a great job presenting, but I don't see how collecting little square pieces of paper with dry glue on the back could be as much fun as they say. I wonder if Robert will try to steal any when they're passed his way (I'm definitely keeping an eye on him).

Ms. Grackle calls up Kristina and Louise next. They present their cake-decorating project and even brought in a giant, green turtle cake to share. They took step-by-step pictures of everything they did to make their turtle cake and taped their pictures to a display board, like me and Billy did. Their pictures turned out okay, but when they see ours, they'll be wishing they had an Uncle Jay like we do.

When Kristina and Louise hand out pieces of their turtle cake, I silently pray that Robert gets the tail. But then I feel guilty because I'm supposed to be a new creation (but since I'm new at this whole God thing, it's probably going to take me a little more time to get it right).

Ms. Grackle calls us next. Billy and I walk to the front of the room and lean our picture display against the chalkboard so everyone can see. We take turns sharing about our ecotone and how we made suet cakes and hummingbird nectar, and how Pastor Henry helped us make bluebird houses. We talk about the different kinds of plants the birds and butterflies like. We tell them about everyone who shared plants. We tell them everything—except for our pinky swear. When we're done, Billy asks if anyone has a question. Mr. Sparrow raises his hand. "Can anyone go to the birding place?"

Billy answers, "Yes. My parents own the land, and everyone's welcome. River and I actually made the birding place for the whole community. We want everyone to enjoy it."

All of a sudden, Robert stands and walks right up to our display. He doesn't bother to raise his hand. He gets real close and then points to the picture of a chickadee that's eating seeds from the wooden bird feeder. "What are those shiny little round things all over your bird feeder?" he says. "If you ask me, they look like BBs."

My heart sinks, and it's hard for me to breathe. Billy looks my way for a second, but for some reason he doesn't seem flustered. He walks over to the picture and gets real close, just like Robert did. Then he says, "They're probably little dots of paint. That feeder used to be in my dad's workshop, so it could've accidently been splashed when he was painting."

Robert walks back to his half seat, sits down, and clenches his fists. Then he asks another question and still doesn't bother to raise his hand. "So," he says, "how long do birds live, anyways?"

I look at Billy, not believing this is real. I'm so scared that all I can do is stand as still and motionless as a dead bird.

Billy answers calmly, "We actually didn't include information about the lifespan of birds in our project. But I do know that most small birds, like the ones that come to the birding place, live approximately one year." Billy shrugs his right shoulder. "But then again," he says, "if you're asking about all birds, an albatross will often live longer than most humans."

Billy isn't pale or shaky, but Robert's face looks tight and red, and it doesn't seem like he has any plans to stop. He asks another question, "Then tell me, when them small birds die, what do they die from?"

"Good question," Billy answers. "Most often they die from natural causes...like old age, sickness, or from extremes in temperature or weather." Billy never says they die when some creep shoots them with a BB gun.

Finally, Mr. Sparrow tells Robert he needs to give other students a chance. Robert squirms in his seat and can't seem to hold still (I feel sorry for Angelina who's on the other half of the seat).

* * *

Mr. Sparrow's class leaves after the last presentation, and Ms. Grackle waves goodbye to them. Then she smiles her shiny, purple-lipstick smile and says she has one more surprise for us. And since there's no possible way it could be worse than her first surprise, I actually feel a bit of excitement (but then I'm not sure what to think since she wore that purple dress to school). Anything could happen.

Ms. Grackle clicks her shimmering purple self over to the phone and calls Mr. Augur. "Bring it on down," she says and then stands in the doorway all excited (like a kid waiting for Christmas) and leaves us hanging in suspense.

Two minutes later Mr. Augur walks into the room carrying the biggest pizza box I've ever seen. The smell of pepperoni finds its way to my nose.

Ms. Grackle clicks over to her desk, bends down, and pulls out a bag from underneath. I'm expecting her grape jelly dress to burst a seam, but she stands back up without disaster and places seven big bottles of soda next to the pizza. She arranges them in an arch like a rainbow—cherry-*red*, *orange*, lemon-*yellow*, lime-*green*, *blue*-berry, passion-fruit the color of *indigo*, and *violet* grape (she's obviously been talking with Mr. Grebes, our science teacher who just finished teaching us about spectrums and Roy G. Biv). Sometimes teachers can be so weird.

Ms. Grackle smiles and tells us again how proud she is of us, but I can't keep myself from staring at her mouth. I think about telling her she has a hunk of green turtle frosting right in the corner, where her purple lips meet, but instead I sink my teeth into the best tasting pizza ever and take a nice long drink of the rainbow.

★ ★ ★

Billy and I walk home from school together, but neither of us says a word about Robert. We kick a stone back and forth instead.

Billy looks my way and asks, "Did you hear the weather report? It's supposed to reach eighty-five degrees tomorrow. That's even hotter than today. I'm definitely wearing shorts to school." I imagine Billy wearing shorts with his pure white socks and brown leather shoes. The thought of it makes me smile. Only Billy could get away with that.

As we turn the corner onto Meadowlark Lane, Billy asks if I can go to the birding place with him. "It's pretty warm," he says. "I'm sure everything's dry. We should fill the birdbath and give the flowers a good soak."

"I wish I could," I tell him, "but I promised Gram I'd go to physical therapy with her. I have to make sure she tells the therapist about her heart attack—if I'm not there, she'll never tell. She'd probably even ask for more exercises, which could be bad for her heart."

"That's okay. Don't worry," he says. "I'll take care of everything. See you tomorrow."

I turn into my driveway, and Billy heads to the birding place. He smiles and waves. I smile back.

* ★ * ★ * ★ * ★ * ★ * ★ * ★ * ★ * ★ * ★ * ★ * ★ *

22

The Color of a Bluebird

*G*ram's therapy place has all kind of neat things. There's a ton of balls, all in different sizes, a set of wooden steps that don't go anywhere but back down again, a row of weight machines, and one very big mirror.

Gram's therapist has her begin by balancing on her right foot while they play catch with a beach ball. Then he tells her to switch to her left foot, and they do the same thing. She's actually doing pretty good and keeps her balance better than I thought. Maybe this guy does know what he's doing.

Next he tells Gram, "Stand up straight and put your heels together. Now point your toes out to the side. Good," he says. "Now squat all the way to the floor and hold two...three...four. Now slowly rise back up." I suddenly have flashbacks from when I was six when Gram dragged me off to ballet class. She made me go every week. She had some crazy idea that I'd transform into a graceful ballerina (I think you can say God changed the course on that one).

So basically Gram's doing grand pliés in first position like I used to do (but at least she doesn't fall over).

I imagine Gram wearing a fluffy white tutu that floats and drifts around her waist, like a big white inner tube. Then as I look at her entire body (including her bright orange tennis shoes and big bottom sticking out), I have a funny thought. She looks an awful lot like Paddles.

The next thing the therapist tells Gram to do is run five miles on the treadmill. Obviously he doesn't realize Gram is well over sixty. And since she hasn't bothered to tell him about her heart attack, I do (which is exactly why I had to be here). Gram gives me one of her looks. "Oh fiddlesticks," she says. "I'm stronger than ten workhorses tied together."

Gram's physical therapist looks directly at her. "Mrs. Nuthatch, you failed to tell me very important information. Now listen," he says. "You're not to do any further exercise until I talk with your doctor. You're to go home and rest until you hear back from me. Do you understand?"

Gram answers with a *humph* and then waddles out of the therapy room with a pout. After she pays her bill, we head to the parking lot where she decides to skip along the pavement like a skidder-bug on water, weaving in and out and between every row of cars she sees until she finds Tilly.

I try so hard to keep her safe.

* * *

When we get home, it's already time for supper. Then out of the blue, Gram comes up with another crazy idea and says she's going to teach me how to make chipped beef on toast. She says it's high time I learn how to cook a decent meal. So, she sits down at the table and spits out orders like a drill sergeant. "Get your ingredients and line 'em up on the counter," she says. "Come on, Sugar Pie, start marching. You're gonna need that little package of chipped beef in the fridge, four pieces of bread, a half of a stick of butter, a quarter cup of flour, a few shakes of pepper, and two cups of milk."

I march around the kitchen doing exactly as she says. I tear open the package of chipped beef and break it into little pieces. I set it aside. Next, I melt the butter in a pan and stir in the flour along with a few shakes of pepper (one time when I was little, I sniffed pepper so hard I sneezed seventeen times in a row—that was one of the dumber things I've done). Then I slowly add the milk and stir until it gets real smooth and creamy. Finally I add the chipped beef. Then I let it simmer while I make the toast.

Gram gets up to set the table (I swear she can't sit still for more than three minutes). When everything's done, I place two pieces of toast on each plate and then drop one big scoop of creamy chipped beef right in the middle.

Gram takes the first bite. "Well, whizbang!" she shouts. "That's the best tasting chipped beef on toast I've ever had!"

And Gram never tells a lie.

★ ★ ★

I clear and scrape the dishes while Gram washes. Tonight she doesn't relevé, so I wonder if she's feeling okay. As I wipe the table, there's a knock on the door, and Pastor Henry pokes his head in. "Hello, River," he says and then notices Gram, "and hello to you as well, Mrs. Nuthatch. I tried calling but forgot that your phone's not working. So since it's such a beautiful evening, I thought I'd walk over. I need to get Billy. His brothers and sisters are waiting for him. You know how much they love it when he reads their bedtime story."

For a minute I can't do anything but stare at him. Then I get this awful feeling inside, kind of like someone's sucked all the air out of me...like I know something terrible has happened. I look at Pastor Henry and shake my head while three small words come out of my mouth, "Billy's not here."

Pastor Henry looks at me with an empty face. "What do you mean, 'he's not here'?"

Even though it's not what he wants to hear, I have to answer. "We walked home from school together, but then I went to physical therapy with Gram, and he went to the birding place."

Then Pastor Henry says, "Oh, God," (not like a swear word—because pastors aren't allowed to swear—but like he's calling on God in a very big way) and he takes off running.

I try catching up to him, but my feet are so heavy. They feel like they have big bags of birdseed tied to them. I run in slow motion. From behind I hear Gram huffing and puffing. I try running faster, but I can't.

Finally I reach the end of the trail when I see Pastor Henry looking over the edge of the riverbank—then he disappears down the bank. I run to the edge. Even though I don't want to, I make myself look down. Pastor Henry picks up Billy, cradles him in his arms like a baby, and cries harder than I've ever heard anyone cry. And Billy's not moving. His body is limp and lifeless, just like his dangling arm...and he's the color of a bluebird.

23

* *

Gather at the River

wo days later, Gram and I put our dresses on. This is the first time I've been out of my pajamas since Billy died. Gram makes me carry a purse and tells me to put a handful of tissues in it. But since we never have any, I grab a string of toilet paper. She probably thinks I'm going to cry, but I'm not.

We walk down our driveway and make our way along Meadow-lark Lane to the birding place. Billy would be happy to know his service is at our special place, the place where we became friends, where we prayed for miracles, and where we learned about birds and butterflies and about sharing and keeping secrets...and even life and death.

Scattered all over our ecotone are hundreds of people who've come to honor him. The sun's shining, and the birds have come to sing for him. I try telling myself this is a bad dream, but even that isn't helpful.

Pastor Henry stands at the edge of the river, right in front of everyone like he does at church. He speaks loud so everyone can hear. I feel like this isn't real, like I'm not even here. I want to jump on Gram's big white inner tube and float down the river and never come back. She puts her arm on my shoulders so I don't, and I put an arm around Mrs. Whippoorwill, who is so sad. I want to take her sadness away and make everything all right, like it used to be. And it would be if I'd gone with Billy instead of going with Gram.

I should have helped him water the flowers. I could have grabbed him before he fell. I could have kept him safe. Why wasn't I there for him? I was too busy trying to keep Gram safe. Why do I always have to keep everyone safe?

This must be the hardest thing Pastor Henry has ever done. His voice is shaky, and he swallows a lot. "Billy knew where he was going. He confirmed his faith last Sunday. He just didn't know when he was going. He didn't realize it would be so soon. None of us know when our last day will be or when we'll take our last breath. Life doesn't come with a forecast or with details all wrapped up in a neat little package."

That makes me think about the package of chipped beef and how smooth and creamy the sauce was. Why am I thinking about chipped beef on toast when my best friend is dead and his father is telling everyone about life and death? I'm just so glad Billy came forward with me and Gram because now I know for sure he's in heaven. I wonder if he can see us. I wonder if he wishes I was there to help him. I wonder what it felt like to die. Did he have to wait a long time all alone, or did he die right away? I hope he wasn't scared. And then I feel happy because I know Billy would never have been scared. He was brave. He didn't even let Robert scare him during our presentation. Billy would never be afraid to die.

I look around the birding place at all the people from church, the kids from school, our teachers, and Mr. Augur, who must be sweating in his wool suit coat (it's a good thing I'm not standing next to him because I wouldn't want to be smelling mothballs when I'm trying to say goodbye to my best friend).

I look up at one of the bluebird houses and see little pieces of blue yarn hanging from the hole. If that were Billy's house, he'd have every last piece of blue yarn tucked neatly inside.

Pastor Henry keeps talking. "We don't know why things happen the way they do, but we need to trust God that he has a purpose for everything. We must trust him in our pain—even when we think we can't."

Mrs. Bunting's watching two hummingbirds sip nectar from her blue phlox. She wipes her eyes, and Mr. Bunting stands close beside her, holding her hand.

Pastor Henry says, "There's something very important that Billy would want every one of you here to know. He'd want you to know how easy God has made it for us to get to heaven." So that's what Pastor Henry does. He tells everyone about God's sacrifice, about being a new creation, about forgiveness, and how we have a heavenly Father who loves us more than anyone ever could.

The sorrowful cry of a mourning dove breaks the silence. "*Wh' hooo hoo hoo hooo*," he calls, looking for someone who'll mourn with him.

My heart cries back, "I will-will-will."

Pastor Henry asks everyone to join him in singing "Shall We Gather at the River." We don't have hymnals at the birding place, and I couldn't sing anyway—the lump in my throat is too big. But everyone else in Birdsong seems to know the words. I fiddle with my purse and pull out a piece of toilet paper. My eyes are only watery because the sun's shining in them. I wipe them dry while everyone sings.

> Shall we gather at the river,
> Where bright angel feet have trod,
> With its crystal tide forever
> Flowing by the throne of God?
>
> Yes, we'll gather at the river,
> The beautiful, the beautiful river;
> Gather with the saints at the river
> That flows by the throne of God.

On the margin of the river,
Washing up its silver spray,
We will talk and worship ever,
All the happy golden day.

Ere we reach the shining river,
Lay we ev'ry burden down;
Grace our spirits will deliver,
And provide a robe and crown.

At the smiling of the river,
Mirror of the Savior's face,
Saints, whom death will never sever,
Lift their songs of saving grace.

Soon we'll reach the shining river,
Soon our pilgrimage will cease;
Soon our happy hearts will quiver
With the melody of peace.

Yes, we'll gather at the river,
The beautiful, the beautiful river;
Gather with the saints at the river
That flows by the throne of God.

Pastor Henry looks out across our ecotone and thanks everyone for coming. "This couldn't have been a better way to celebrate Billy's life. Thanks for sharing it with us." Then he takes a hanky from his back pocket and blows his nose. He honks louder than a Canada goose and scares a bluebird right out of its house. Billy would have laughed hysterically.

Everyone else leaves because only Billy's family is invited to the cemetery. Mrs. Whippoorwill reminds me and Gram that we're family.

Before we leave, I walk over to the edge of the river and look down. I want to see Billy there, calling up to me. "Hey, River, can you give me a hand please? I'm fine! Just toss the rope and pull me up." But instead of seeing Billy, I see something long and shiny glistening in the sun. It's hanging off a root. I bend down and have to lie on my stomach to reach it, but I'm not worried about my dress getting dirty. I stretch my arm as far as I can and grab hold of it. It's after I get back up and open my hand that I realize what I'm holding. My body suddenly feels scared and shaky as I picture Robert walking along the river with his leather wallet sticking out of his pocket and hooked to that long, silver chain—a piece of it now in my hand. As I quickly wrap it in toilet paper and tuck it in my purse, our pinky-swear words spin over and over in my head. "Pinky, pinky, grip real tight. A promise told will not lose hold, but break your word, you'll break our bond. It's pinky swear or death beware."

24

Yellow Roses

Pastor Henry drives us to the cemetery in his big white van. He follows close behind the black hearse, where Billy's coffin is.

Little Forrest calls out, "Mama, where's Billy? How come he not here?" She tells him he's in heaven now, helping God. I close my eyes and imagine Billy making a birding place in heaven, right along a beautiful river that flows gently with silver water. There are bluebirds all around him. Their feathers are the truest blue, their wings are like angels' wings, and they're singing songs that could make the saddest person feel hopeful.

Forrest cries out again, "Mama, I want Billy."

She rubs his back. "I know, Forrest. I know."

* * *

At the cemetery four men, dressed in suits, pull Billy's casket out of the hearse and carry it to his grave. They set him right beside the big hole. It doesn't seem like Billy could really be in a casket. I want to open the lid so Billy can pop out and yell, "Surprise!" But Billy would never do such a dumb thing. But if he did, you can be sure Pastor Henry would make him do more than polish church pews.

Billy's grandparents, aunts, uncles, and all his cousins are here too. Uncle Jay didn't bring his camera (I guess people don't take pictures at funerals—dead people don't smile, and neither does anyone else who has to be there). But it might not be a bad idea to have a few pictures because what if a few days from now, or even in a week or two, you start wondering if that person really is dead. You might think it's just been a bad dream, so at least pictures would be proof.

Pastor Henry stands by Billy's casket and opens his Bible. "Psalm 23. The LORD is my shepherd; I shall not want. He makes me lie down in green pastures. He leads me beside still waters. He restores my soul. He leads me in paths of righteousness for his name's sake. Even though I walk through the valley of the shadow of death, I will fear no evil, for you are with me; your rod and your staff, they comfort me. You prepare a table before me in the presence of my enemies; you anoint my head with oil; my cup overflows. Surely goodness and mercy shall follow me all the days of my life, and I shall dwell in the house of the LORD forever." He closes his Bible.

"Billy was a gift from God," he says, "a gift that was with us for twelve short years. The earthly part of me wants to shout, 'He wasn't with us long enough! I'm not ready to say goodbye!' But then I hear the quiet voice of God say, 'My ways are higher than yours. Trust me. I will be with you.' Will we miss him? Of course we will. Will we feel pain we think we can't endure? Without a doubt. Will God give us the strength to make it through? He made a promise."

Pastor Henry bows his head. "Dear heavenly Father, we thank you for Billy. He loved his family, his friends, and all your creation. We ask that you be with us. Give us the strength to go on. We thank you that we have your promise of seeing him again someday."

Billy's headstone is real big, and it has a picture of him carved

on the front. He's smiling his crooked smile. Next to his picture,
it says:

WILLIAM FORREST WHIPPOORWILL
Born November 11, 1970
He went home to be with his heavenly Father on
June 15, 1983
Son of Henry and Elizabeth
Oldest brother of Nathan, Daniel, Bethany,
Hannah, Rebecca, and Forrest
Best friend of River

I start crying and can't stop. Uncle Jay pulls me close. He feels
like a warm flannel blanket wrapped around me so tight that nothing could ever hurt me. I don't want him to ever let go.

At the very bottom of Billy's headstone is a Bible verse:

Romans 14:8
If we live, we live to the Lord,
and if we die, we die for the Lord.
So then, whether we live or whether we die,
we are the Lord's.

The men dressed in suits lower Billy's casket into the ground.
We each take a handful of dirt, and one by one, toss it on top of his
casket. I hate the empty sound. I'm glad Billy can't hear it. It must
be dark and lonely in there, but Billy doesn't even know it. Only
the outside part of Billy is there—the dead part, the part that can't
feel or see or move or breathe. The living part of Billy is in heaven,
hanging out with God.

After everyone throws their dirt, we walk around his headstone
to the other side where there's more writing. I run my fingers over
the words. They feel cold and lonely and hopeful all at the same
time. My fingers trace each word:

> All things bright and beautiful,
> All creatures great and small,
> All things wise and wonderful,
> The Lord God made them all.
>
> Each little flower that opens,
> Each little bird that sings,
> He made their glowing colors,
> He made their tiny wings.

I begin to think about wings, not the kind birds have, but the big, flowing kind that angels have, and how they let you fly. If everyone in heaven gets wings, I hope Billy gets two strong ones that work. I want him to be able to fly.

Mrs. Whippoorwill hands each little Whippoorwill a yellow rose. She says they represent the promise of a new beginning. She hands me one too. Then one at a time, each little Whippoorwill goes over to Billy's grave and drops their rose in. After Mrs. Whippoorwill helps Forrest, I walk over and let mine go. "Goodbye, Billy," I say. "See you in heaven." We walk away, singing the last part of "Amazing Grace."

> Amazing grace! how sweet the sound!
> That saved a wretch like me!
> I once was lost, but now am found;
> Was blind, but now I see.
>
> The Lord has promised good to me,
> His Word my hope secures;
> He will my shield and portion be,
> As long as life endures.
>
> Yea, when this flesh and heart shall fail,
> And mortal life shall cease,

I shall possess within the veil,
A life of joy and peace.

When we've been there ten thousand years,
Bright, shining as the sun,
We've no less days to sing God's praise
Than when we first begun.

* * * * * * * * * * * * * * * * * * * *

25

Little Bird on My Lip

*g*ram's clock struck midnight a long time ago. It's pitch black, and I'm lying in bed with thoughts racing around my head like lab rats in a maze trying to find their way out. Every thought is of Billy, and I can't find a place where everything is quiet. I think about Pastor Henry and Mrs. Whippoorwill and how all the little Whippoorwills are going to miss Billy every night when he's not there to read to them. Nathan will have to take over. He's the oldest now.

I think about me and wonder what I'll do without him. I think about the birding place, and then I remember the chain. How did Robert's chain end up hanging off a root? Was he fishing there? He couldn't have been—he said he'd never stand on that edge. Then I think about how mean and strange he acted when me and Billy did our presentation. He was so mad at Billy for not telling about the BBs. Robert's been mad enough before to throw a rock through a church window. I wonder if he was mad enough to push Billy over the edge of the Meadowlark River.

All the pieces shift around my head and slowly fit together like a puzzle. But there's one piece missing—Billy. Robert has so much darkness in him that I think he could've pushed him. And if he did, Billy would have reached for something to grab onto but only got hold of a piece of Robert's chain. It could have broken, fallen off his wallet, and got caught on the root when it dropped over the edge. Robert would've gotten scared and run away. But one thing he doesn't know—God was there and saw what happened. God was with Billy the whole time. He didn't die alone.

I think about telling Pastor Henry everything, but I pinky swore with Billy that I'd never tell a soul about Robert breaking the window, and I'm not sure if our pinky swear includes what Robert could have done this time.

It's still dark, and Gram's clock strikes three.

* * *

The sunlight's trying to creep past my curtains and make me wake up. I tell it to go away. I reach for a bobby pin to clip them together. I won't let it in, so I close my eyes tight. If I keep them shut, I won't have to get up. I won't have to find out how awful it's going to be without Billy.

Gram knocks on my door and pokes her head in. "You gonna sleep all day, Sugar Pie?" She waits for me to answer, but I can't. "The morning's come and gone, so if you wait much more, it'll come and go again."

My voice is dry and crackly. "That's fine with me."

Gram waddles over and sits on my bed. "Now, Sugar Pie, if you keep pouting like that, a little bird is gonna come land on your lip." She puts her hand on my back and rubs in a circle. It feels so good I cry. Gram whispers, "It'll be okay, Sugar Pie. It's just gonna take some time." Then she rubs my head. "You're one tough cookie, Sugar Pie, and you're gonna be okay."

I tell myself Gram never lies.

26

Evidence

Two days pass and I'm still not okay. Gram lets me stay home from school. I miss Billy so much, and our pinky swear won't leave me alone. I worry what will happen if I break it.

Gram and I sit at the kitchen table, finishing off her tin of chocolate-chip cookies, when Pastor Henry walks up our driveway. He's carrying Gram's casserole dish. She made the Whippoorwills her famous goulash and peas concoction. That's what everyone does when someone you love dies. They feed you, hoping it will make you feel better. Gram mixed the goulash and peas all together since that's her way of cooking fancy. But I'll bet the Whippoorwills liked it because they're used to having food all mixed together.

Gram opens the door and invites Pastor Henry in. He looks worn out, like he needs to sleep for a whole week without anyone bothering him. "The casserole was delicious," he tells Gram. "You make it just like Elizabeth."

Gram smiles and nods her head. It's kind of awkward when someone dies because you never know what to say. There might be magic punch, but there aren't any magic words that will change the way things are. I can tell Gram's not sure what to say, but Pastor Henry tries making her feel comfortable. "We appreciate your kindness, Mrs. Nuthatch, and wanted to get your dish back right away."

Then he comes over and pulls me in tight and close, just like

Uncle Jay did. For a little while, it feels like everything's going to be all right. He keeps his arms around me while he talks. "Thank you for being a friend to Billy. He always talked about how much you meant to him." Then he loosens his hug, reaches in his pocket, and pulls out a folded piece of paper that looks like it went through the laundry. "This was in Billy's pocket," he says and places it in my hand. "He meant for you to have it."

My whole body shakes. I want to read it, but I need to be by myself when I do, so I just keep it folded and hold onto it real tight. I never want to lose it. I look up at Pastor Henry, not one hundred percent sure I want to say anything, but my mouth opens, and the words come out all on their own. "I have something for you too," I say, and then I run to my room. I open my sock drawer and take out the folded piece of toilet paper. I tuck Billy's letter in my diary, right between my special feathers. I hurry back and hand the toilet paper to Pastor Henry. "I think you should know about this."

He unfolds the paper and pulls out the broken piece of chain. That's when everything rushes out of me like a raging river, and I feel like I'm barely hanging on to Gram's white inner-tube, spinning far, far away down the Meadowlark River. I shake my head and try to talk. "Billy and I pinky swore, but I think I have to break it so you'll know what the chain means. Robert is the one who threw the rock through the church window, and he killed all those birds, and he kept bothering Billy the day we did our presentation. He was so mad at Billy, and that was the same day Billy fell off the edge of the riverbank, and..."

Pastor Henry leads me to the couch and makes me sit down. He tells me to take a deep breath, then makes me start from the beginning. I tell him everything—every little detail.

Pastor Henry sits on the couch beside me. He doesn't say a word. He doesn't move. I think he's letting everything sink into his brain, trying to make sense of it. He runs his hands over his head and looks at me. "You did the right thing, River. You needed to break your pinky swear in a situation like this." The knot I've felt inside my chest starts to untangle, and I feel like I can breathe again. "River," he says, "would you go to the sheriff's office with me? The authorities need to know."

I nod.

Gram puts her arm around me. "You want me to come too, Sugar Pie? I wanna make sure they catch that Killdeer boy."

"That's okay, Gram. I can do this. I need to be brave for Billy."

$$\ast\ \ast\ \ast$$

Pastor Henry holds the door as we walk through the main entrance of the police station. It's a small brick building with an American flag flying outside. It's flying at half-mast in honor of Billy. I stay as close to Pastor Henry as I can. I've never been inside Birdsong's sheriff's office before, or any other sheriff's office for that matter.

Pastor Henry says hello to the secretary and asks if we could speak with Sheriff Peterson.

The secretary, Ms. Pintail, points to the chairs beside her desk. "Please have a seat while I get the sheriff."

While we wait, Pastor Henry assures me I have nothing to be afraid of. He says all I need to do is tell Sheriff Peterson everything I told him. But then I start to worry. What if Sheriff Peterson brings Robert to his office for questioning, and he ends up being innocent? Robert will know who told on him, and then he'll come after me. Billy's words echo in my head, "...but break your word, you'll break our bond. It's pinky swear or death beware."

Ms. Pintail's voice startles me. "Sheriff Peterson says you can head back to his office." Pastor Henry nods his head and thanks her.

Sheriff Peterson greets us. "Good morning, Pastor. You've been in my thoughts. What can I do for you?"

Pastor Henry puts his hand on my shoulder. "This is River Starling, Billy's friend. She confided in me this morning and shared information I think you need to be aware of."

Sheriff Peterson tells us to have a seat as he pulls a small spiral notebook and pen from his shirt pocket. He asks me questions about the broken stained glass window and how Robert behaved during our presentation. He asks if we actually saw Robert shoot the birds and if he ever actually threatened Billy or me. I answer every question as best I can.

Then Sheriff Peterson takes the piece of silver chain from Pastor Henry and inspects it carefully, holding it up to the sunlight coming through his window. He slips it into a plastic bag, rummages through his desk to find a permanent marker, and then writes "Killdeer Case" on it. He closes his notebook and grabs his hat off the hook. "As soon as I have any information, I'll call. But until then, don't say a word about this to anyone. Do you understand, River? Not a soul." I promise him I won't, and then he rushes out of his office before Pastor Henry and I have a chance to stand up.

As we walk out the back exit, we hear his siren and the sound of tires screeching. The smell of burnt rubber hits us.

27

The Letter

Pastor Henry drops me off at the end of my driveway. Gram's standing in the doorway waiting for me. "Come on in, Sugar Pie. Lunch is waiting." She pulls out my chair and says, "Now, you have a seat and a bite to eat and tell me all about it." Gram has a vase of wildflowers sitting in the middle of the table. She made a huge stack of peanut butter and fluff sandwiches with banana slices tucked inside, and she mixed two tall glasses of chocolate milk with ice cubes (that's Gram's way of trying to make things better). She sits across the table from me and folds her hands. "Now, you go on ahead and tell me everything about the police station, just like it happened."

So I do.

"Well," Gram says, "it sounds like that Sheriff Peterson's got a good head on his shoulders." Then she guzzles her chocolate milk and wipes her mouth on her sleeve. "As I live and breathe, I just want to see justice." Gram shakes her head. "That Killdeer boy sounds crazier than a run-over dog. I just hope to God that Sheriff Peterson finds enough evidence to prove what that boy did." Then she shakes her head, yawns, and decides to take an afternoon snooze. I get my diary and walk to the birding place.

As I push the branches away and turn onto the trail, I look across the road at the Whippoorwill's mailbox. I remember Billy standing there the first day we started our project. I picture the seed packages sticking out of his pockets and remember him holding that huge bag of birdseed. But all I did was complain about how early in the morning it was. It seems so long ago.

* * *

I sit on the log, which is all soft and covered with moss, and take a deep breath in. I look across the birding place. The grass is still matted down where everyone stood for Billy's service. This is actually the first time I've been here alone. It's so peaceful. The birds are singing, and there are butterflies everywhere. There's even a chipmunk under the feeder, stuffing dropped seeds into his cheeks. No wonder Mrs. Bunting likes coming here. I just hope she doesn't come today. I need to be alone.

I open my diary and take out Billy's letter. Then it hits me. If this was in his pocket when he died, he must have planned on giving it to me after school that day. That's why he wanted me to go to the birding place with him. Why did I promise Gram I'd go to physical therapy with her? She would have been fine without me. And if I'd said yes to Billy, he'd still be here with me.

I close my eyes and try to swallow the lump in my throat. "I'm so sorry, Billy. I should have gone with you. I should have been there to save you." But then I remember what Pastor Henry said: "Who by worrying can add a single moment to your life?...therefore, don't worry."

"God," I whisper, "please help me be strong." I wipe my eyes and unfold the letter. When I see his handwriting, I can't help but smile. It's a good thing I finally learned to read chicken scratch.

Dear River:

Since God knows everything, I figured

he'd be able to help us come up with something you can tell people when they ask about your name. And I don't think I ever told you, but I think your name is awesome, just like you are. Anyway, last night I prayed and asked God to help me find a special Bible verse, thinking it might lead us somewhere. And you won't believe this, but right after I prayed, I opened my Bible to John 7:38. I could hardly believe what I read: Jesus said, "Whoever believes in me, as the Scripture has said, 'Out of his heart will flow rivers of living water.'"

Isn't that amazing? The word river is right in it! And since you believe in God, that means you have rivers of living water flowing from your heart. But don't worry. He's not talking about a real river. He's talking about his Spirit. Jesus used "rivers of living water" as a symbol for his Spirit. So just think...you,

River Starling, have God's Spirit flowing from your heart.

And then I thought, since God is your heavenly Father, you could even say your father named you, and, technically, I don't think that would be considered a lie, but we could ask my dad just to make sure.

If you like this idea, you could practice saying it so the next time someone asks about your name, you can tell them. And it'll probably feel like you've known it all your life. But if you don't like it, that's okay. We'll think of something else.

Your friend,

Billy

I whisper out loud, "I like it, Billy. I like it very much." Then I write it in my diary.

> John 7:38. Whoever believes in me, as the Scripture has said, "Out of his heart will flow rivers of living water."

I write it over and over until I have it memorized.

I imagine Billy sitting on the log beside me. I pretend we're meeting each other for the first time. He tells me his name is Billy, and then he asks what mine is. He tells me he's glad I came to see the new birding place, and then he asks why my name is River. I tell him my father named me after a Bible verse where Jesus says, "Whoever believes in me, as the Scripture has said, 'Out of his heart will flow rivers of living water.'" And then, if Billy wonders what that means, I'll do exactly what Pastor Henry does. I'll tell him all about God, and how he can be sure he'll go to heaven. I'll tell him how great it is to have a heavenly Father who loves you more than anyone ever has or ever could—even enough to die for you.

I lean back, press my hands against the soft, cool moss, and look up at the sky. It's a hopeful kind of blue, like a robin's egg, and it's filled with white cotton clouds drifting all about. I try seeing beyond them, and wonder if that's where heaven begins.

28

* * * * * * * * * * * * * * * * * * *

Uncle Jay's Picture

My alarm clock moans like a sad cow. I hit it so hard it falls off my nightstand. I roll over, wanting to go back to sleep, but my calendar's staring me in the face. It's July third—exactly eighteen days since Billy died. But at least it's a Sunday, and I'll see the Whippoorwills.

I throw on a skirt and try brushing my hair (but some things are just impossible). Gram's already banging around the kitchen, and the smell of burnt toast has drifted all the way to my room. I follow it down the hall.

Gram's waving her dishrag to clear the smoke. "Morning, Sugar Pie."

"Good morning, Gram." I sit at the table and stare at the square black thing sitting on my plate.

"Sorry about the toast, Sugar Pie. That blasted toaster's on its last leg. Just go ahead and scrape off the black. It'll be okay."

Gram waves her dishrag a few more times and then grabs the Sunday paper. "Well, I'll be jiggered!" she shouts and then waddles over to my side of the table. She pokes the headlines with her finger and says, "Would you look at this, Sugar Pie? Killdeer Boy Guilty!" Gram presses the paper flat and continues.

Robert Killdeer, age thirteen, of Birdsong, West Virginia, pleads guilty to the untimely death of William Whippoorwill, age twelve. Both boys attended

135

Birdsong Middle School. William and his friend, River Starling, had been working on a school project at the Meadowlark River, where they built a birding place for their community. On the evening of June 15th, William was found there, where he had fallen over the cliff along the river. William was pronounced dead at the scene.

After Sheriff Peterson's in-depth investigation, Robert Killdeer confessed. He said he and William were standing at the edge of the river when they began to argue. He said he was angry and pushed William but never meant for him to fall over the edge and die. When Robert was asked what they had been arguing about, he said he couldn't remember. William's mother, Elizabeth Whippoorwill, commented, "William will always be alive in our hearts, and we miss him more than words can express...It's only because of God that we live with hope. We know we'll see him again." When William's father, Pastor Henry Whippoorwill, was asked how he felt toward the convicted, he said, "God knows the hearts of all people, and regardless of the good or bad we've done, he loves us. I can only pray Robert will get the help he needs and that he's able to become the young person God intended."

Robert is being held in a locked facility for wayward boys where he will receive psychological testing and rehabilitation. No release date has been set at this time.

Gram looks at me like I should jump up and down with excitement. "That's great, Gram, but it doesn't bring Billy back. Nothing can." She rubs my head and tries combing her fingers through my hair.

Gram rolls the paper into a log and holds it up. "You think Pastor Henry has seen this?"

"I doubt it. The Whippoorwills are real busy on Sunday mornings."

"Well, let's save them a bit of time. Instead of having them pick us up here this morning, we'll go there. Besides, I think I hear the wind calling us that way. Let's go, Sugar Pie."

I set our dishes in the sink, and Gram wipes the crumbs off the table and onto the floor. She tucks the Sunday paper under her arm and bursts out the screen door. I follow in her tailwind.

We reach the end of our driveway and turn toward the Whippoorwill's when Gram breaks into a jog. "What are you doing, Gram? Did you forget you've got your heels on?" Gram skids to a stop, takes off her shoes, and tucks them under the paper. She starts jogging again. Her stockings will be in shreds by the time we get there.

As we reach the front steps, the warm smell of cinnamon rolls wraps around me like a hug and makes me think of Uncle Jay.

Gram bangs on the door. Pastor Henry greets us and says, "What a nice surprise! And perfect timing. Elizabeth just pulled cinnamon rolls out of the oven. Come on in."

We walk in, and I can't believe my eyes. Uncle Jay is sitting at the table. But not for long because he jumps up, runs over, and scoops me into a big bear hug. "It's good to see you, River."

"It's good to see you too, Uncle Jay." And for some reason, my eyes feel warm, and I have to wipe them. "I didn't expect to see you this morning," I say.

"No one did. It wasn't until last night that I decided to surprise everyone. I threw a few things in my bag, jumped into my car, and got here just a few minutes ago—just in time for cinnamon rolls."

Mrs. Whippoorwill smiles and pulls out chairs for me and

Gram. "Sit down and help yourself. There's more than enough for everyone."

I sit between Uncle Jay and little Forrest, who reaches out and touches me with sticky fingers. He smiles and pats my arm. "Riber," he says.

Gram takes a bite of her cinnamon roll and holds up the Sunday paper for Pastor Henry to see. "I brought this in case you hadn't seen it yet."

Pastor Henry answers, "That was thoughtful, Mrs. Nuthatch, but we actually had a visit from Sheriff Peterson last night. He told us about Robert confessing. And you can bet that news changed my sermon this morning. I'll be sharing about forgiveness instead of Moses."

Gram looks confused. "Forgiveness? As in forgiving that Killdeer boy?"

Pastor Henry nods. "It's probably not what you expected, but that is what I mean. It might be hard to imagine, but in God's eyes, Robert is no different than any one of us. We're all imperfect. We all make mistakes. I believe God wants us to reach out to Robert and show him the kind of love that God shows us. We need to show Robert what forgiveness is, even if we don't feel like it. I've been learning that forgiveness isn't a choice, and it's not a feeling either…It's a command."

Gram takes a bite of her cinnamon roll, swallows, and says, "Humph."

Pastor Henry reaches out and squeezes Gram's shoulder. "We'll talk more about it at church."

Uncle Jay looks at Gram. "You know, Mrs. Nuthatch, Billy said you were interested in seeing a picture of mine—the one I carry in my wallet. I can't imagine why you'd want to see it. It's pretty beat up after all those years, but, nonetheless, if you're still interested, I've got it right here."

Gram sets her coffee mug down. "I'd like to have a look cuz there's something puzzling going on, and I think I hear the rustle of the wind."

Uncle Jay takes the picture from his wallet. As he hands it my way to give to Gram, I take a look. "Wow, Uncle Jay," I say. "This was your wife?"

He nods.

"She's so beautiful," I tell him. "And this was your baby?"

He nods again.

"That's strange," I say. "Your baby looks just like a picture Gram has of me when I was little. We have on the same yellow checkered dress and the same necklace with a dangling heart charm. We both have brown curly hair...and the same crooked little smile."

Gram peeks over my shoulder to see the picture. "She's right. The picture I have was taken the day my daughter 'adopted' River. And your picture was taken the day your daughter went missing."

Uncle Jay shakes his head like he's confused. Then he looks at me. "That means—"

Gram doesn't give him a chance to finish. "That means Sheriff Peterson's got two more criminals to catch—my daughter and that knuckleheaded husband of hers."

All of a sudden, everything turns blurry, and my head feels lighter than a helium balloon. Then the next thing I know, I'm lying on the couch, and Uncle Jay's beside me holding a cold cloth across my forehead. He smiles and says, "You're all right, River. You just fainted."

I look at him and smile.

"Do you know what this means?" he says. "It means I'm your father. And because you were friends with Billy, I finally found you." He wraps his arms around me.

I hug him back. "I knew my dad would find me. I just didn't know he would be you."

$\star\,^\star\,_\star\,^\star\,_\star\,^\star\,_\star\,^\star\,_\star\,^\star\,_\star\,^\star\,_\star\,^\star\,_\star\,^\star\,_\star$

Discussion Questions

These questions can be used as a springboard for group discussion:

- At first River isn't happy about moving and would rather stay in Punxsutawney, Pennsylvania. Has there been a time in your life when everything changed from the "known" to the "unknown"? How did you feel? Read Joshua 1:9.

- Gram tells River, "Everything's gotta change sometime." But there's one thing we can be sure of—God never changes. Read Malachi 3:6.

- When River meets William, she assumes he's the class dork based only on his outward appearance. Have you ever judged someone by their outward appearance? Or have you been judged in that way?

- River sings the hymn "It Is Well with My Soul" but isn't sure what the words mean. Look back in chapter 11 and reread the words to that hymn. What do they mean to you? Read Philippians 4:11-12.

- Billy realizes his camera isn't good enough and asks God for help. He tells River, "God is so incredible that even though he has to take care of the big things, he wants to help us with the little things." Read Matthew 6:8.

- After Robert kills the birds, Billy prays for him. Would you have done that? Read Matthew 5:44.

- Sometimes it's hard to understand why God answers our prayers like he does. His answers may not always be what we hope for. Read Jeremiah 29:11.

About the Author

Wendy Dunham is a registered therapist and works with children who have special needs. Although she enjoys writing for children and adults, her passion is writing middle-grade fiction. She is the mother of two adult children and a wonderful son-in-law, who she loves to the moon and back. She enjoys reading, writing, gardening, kayaking, repurposing old furniture, walking, and biking with friends. She is a member of the Society of Children's Book Writers and Illustrators (SCBWI), as well as the local chapter in the Rochester area (RACWI), and Word Weavers International and, again, her local Western New York Chapter.

Her desire is to honor her Creator with whatever it is she's writing about. Whether a poem, an article, a thought-provoking devotional, or a novel, her goal is to share pieces of hope, encouragement, and unconditional love—things we can all use a little bit more of.

She shares her home with Casey, Theo, Smokey, Tiny Tim, and Bentley (her four-legged friends who keep her company).

One of her favorite quotes is by Mother Teresa: "We can do no great things—only small things with great love."

Visit her website at www.wendydunham.net

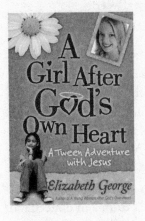

A Girl After God's Own Heart:
A Tween Adventure with Jesus
by Elizabeth George

Bestselling author Elizabeth George follows her popular teen books (more than 400,000 copies sold), including *A Young Woman's Guide to Making Right Choices,* by reaching out to tweens, ages 8 to 12, in *A Girl After God's Own Heart.* Upbeat and positive, Elizabeth provides biblical truths and suggestions so you can thrive. She reaches out to you where you're at and addresses daily issues that concern you, including—

- building real friendships
- talking with parents
- putting Jesus first
- handling schoolwork and activities
- deciding how to dress

A Girl After God's Own Heart will show you how to establish healthy guidelines that honor God, promote your own well-being, and help get the most from this wonderful time in your life.

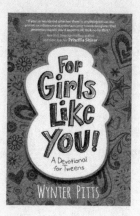

For Girls Like You:
A Devotional for Tweens
by Wynter Pitts

As a tween girl, you have access to an unbelievable amount of media and information with just a simple click of the remote or mouse. Every outlet you turn to attempts to subtly influence your view of yourself and the world you live in. What you believe about yourself directly affects how you live.

Wynter Pitts is founder of *For Girls Like You* magazine, and her new devotional will help you see God's truth and understand the difference it makes in your life. Each daily devotion includes a prayer to help you apply the lesson.